LOKI-ROTICA

BOOKS 1-4

DARRAGHA FOSTER

Loki-Rotica

Darragha Foster

Published by Victory Woman Press 2024. Copyright Darragha Foster. All rights reserved. No part of this publication may be reproduced, stored in a retrieval system, or transmitted in any form or by any means, electronic, mechanical, recording or otherwise, without the prior written permission of the author.

Editor: Marisa Chenery

Cover Artist: Wicked Smart Designs

This is a work of fiction. The characters, incidents and dialogues in this book are of the author's imagination and are not to be construed as real. Any resemblance to actual events or persons, living or dead, is completely coincidental.

Loki-rotica
A Thousand Words on Sex with the Trickster
Darragha Foster

Her

I lay beside Him. He is perfumed with the lingering scent of marijuana and honeysuckle. He carries the smell of freshly mown grass and wild roses. Good whiskey and leather. He is a catalog of olfactory sensuality. His long, dancer's body beckons me to touch. The red fur of His belly trails down to His groin, which displays arousal—for me. A part of me feels sinful and guilty that I want to worship Him. *I will kneel before You and do whatever it is You wish me to do.* For what is a god if not worshipped? Not loved? And I do love Him.

I crave Him. I am addicted to Him. His energy strengthens me. I slowly suck His cock. I want our time together to last. The sooner He climaxes, the sooner He will depart, and I will awaken from trance. I want Him here—with me. Always. Thoughts of the other men and women who call Him "Husband" makes my blood run cold. He doesn't suffer jealousy amongst His People too well. There's enough of Him to go around. I push away thoughts of His other lovers and stoke His shaft. Oh, yes...there's enough to go around.

I breathe in His godhood. It emanates from Him like sweat from a marathoner. There is no odor akin to it in nature for it is the scent of the universe. Of antiquity. Of change. He is a symphony. A choir. A laureate and a magician.

I feel His clever tongue—His silver tongue—slide along my cleft and press into me as easily as his cock might should I not have it in my mouth. My shapeshifter. Though His head rests on my pillows, He has found a way to maximize our time together. I pleasure Him and He returns it to me by way of a probing, soft tongue. I suck harder as he laps at my clitoris. I stroke my hand—no—I must stop this! He must not climax yet. I would have Him as mine and mine alone—longer.

I feel urgency in the big vein of his penis. I have aroused Him fully. I pull away and scramble to place my head next to His. We kiss. I could lose my mind in His kisses. I climb atop Him and press my wetness to His shaft. I masturbate against Him without allowing Him passage. I lean forward to engage Him in another kiss. I touch my tongue against each of the honey-filled scar divots decorating his lips. Sweet scars. Sacred scars. It is a devotional in honor of His finest moments and grievous sufferings. His lips are full and if ever there was a Man to teach all other men how to kiss, it is Him. I am desperate to have Him. To hold Him. Should I slide His thickness into me this very moment, I would never retreat. Never let Him go.

Him

I lay beside her, my mortal wife. My beloved. I find comfort in her bed and solace in her arms. Her offerings of coffee, chocolate, and dark beer honor me. I see beyond her flesh. I see her very essence, and it beckons me to taste. There is no part of her round, fleshy body that I have not taken for My pleasure and hers. A human male might find her too voluptuous of belly and thigh. I think she is perfect. Delicious. One kiss from her lips and I shudder. There is no equal amongst mortal women. There can be no comparison. Of course, I love the one I'm with. For that is My nature. The love between a god and His chosen mortal is sacred. I would consume her so she is always with Me. She is delightful. And skillful. Her sweet mouth on my cock insights fierce passion within Me. I want to fuck her until I can do nothing but sleep for days. The exhausted sleep of a god, well-met by the mouth and pussy and ass of His beloved wife. Ah...she feels my arousal and tastes my seed as it brims to the surface of My cock. Smart girl...she moves to withhold orgasm. Smart woman. She is over forty Earthly years. She's wife to a mortal man, mother to lovely children. A worker and songstress. It was her voice that first led Me to her. Her voice in song and in prayer. There are no words in mortal tongue that can capture the emotion I feel for her. The cry of gulls, purr of a kitten, crackling of fall leaves underfoot. Those are the sounds that best describe what she does to Me.

I want to drink her. I want to lap at her nether regions like a cat before a bowl of cream. Every drop of her precious nectar is holy water. Every muscle spasm brought forth by orgasm is plow point to field—another furrow on consecrated ground. I shall plant My seed deep within her hallowed body and see what rises from her rich, dark soil. What lesson shall I implant? What should she know this day that will help her honor herself more deeply, and Me, more thoroughly?

Her

He laughs at me. He laughs at me and reaches into the liquid heat between our pressed sexual organs. He flicks His tongue. I know what He wants. I roll off Him and go up onto knees and elbows. He does not hesitate. His mouth is upon my quim and ass and His forked tongue penetrates me. The tine in my pussy moves in circular fashion. It's not to taste me. It is to catch my scent. Like a serpent, He uses His forked tongue to breathe in my scent. He will carry the perfume of what He does to me with Him wherever His travels take Him. The second tine penetrates with the thrust and rhythm of a jackhammer. I know He's preparing me to take something of greater girth. I feel my sphincter muscles rebel at the forced stretching. I will them to comply. And then I spill an ocean across His face as I come. He drinks my climax; every drop. He laps at me with a human tongue. Pussy, ass, thighs. I hear Him chuckle. It's His turn.

Him

It doesn't matter how I fill her—so long as I can. And do. Vagina, anus, throat, or even through her breastbone into her heart. I must take her. She incites me to a passionate rage. My cock is a blade through butter; hot iron into snow. The energy which flows between us when engaged in coitus is more than sexual. It is the energy from which all life springs. It is that which creates the force behind the bubbles, which rise from the primordial ooze. It starts with a breath. A single breath, then a thrust and push and moan. What emanates from my throat is a vibration that binds us, confirms us. My orgasm is a juggernaut of godflow. And today, I choose her ass as receptacle of my passionate life-affirming love.

I slap her round bottom. She braces herself, prepared for what comes next. I would never hurt her. Of course I use lubricant.

There is something about the hot, tight chamber of a mortal's ass that is worthy of sonnet. When inside her, I feel safe, not vulnerable to attack. I feel pure love, and its energy feeds my ethereal cells. Her body closes around me like memory foam. An odd comparison, yes, but I swear her flesh remembers me and conforms to me with the vigor of a starving man before a joint of beef.

But I need more of her. All of her.

I hear her thoughts turn to panic when I slide into her ready quim. Ass to vag! Ass to vag! Without a word, for my mouth is most certainly busy upon hers, I reassure her that I am divine and not of this world and should any harmful rectal bacteria pass into her vagina, it is purified and blessed. *I got this, baby. Don't worry. Relax around my cock. Let your body swallow me. Let me fill you.*

I grip her hips and move with wild abandon. My orgasm is of fire and seed. It propels from me like flame from a flamethrower. It burns though her organs and belly, bursts her ribcage and kisses her heart with fire that found its source in the vault of heaven. Her heart steams and boils and burns, and I taste her soul. It is too much for her. A flood of her wetness mixes with my own. It is a bubbling sea of bliss, with perfect ebb and flow. Our combined vims dance. The oldest of dances. It is the music of supplicant to the divine.

She screams my name. "Loki! Loki! I love you. Breathless. I love you. I will do whatever you want me to do. Command me, Husband." A second surge hits. She can no longer speak for the pleasure.

And the fire is quenched. Her passion quelled.

I whisper her name. Again. "I love you, my wife. All I ask...all I need...I would have you love me, nothing more. Promise me that you will always love me."

"Yes." Said through rapid breaths and tears of joy. "Yes."

She melts into closure of her trance.

I must rest now too. I am spent. Expelled. Done. The god is sated. And clever.

For I recognize that for all that I am, I am nothing without her.

Loki-rotica II: In the Shower
Another Thousand Words on Sex with the Trickster
Darragha Foster

Her

Shower time—like the first cup of coffee in the morning—is a gift and blessing. Showers are the magic of hot water, steam, wakefulness. You.

You love shower time. Your excited energy tells me this is so. It is our own private vortex to another realm. Foreplay consists of me stepping out of my undies. I feel Your heat before steam fills the shower stall. I feel Your lips against my ankles as the rush of hot water beats down atop me. I breathe in the steam. I breathe in You. Your spirit envelopes me in a surge of titillation that makes my nether regions quiver. It's no wonder I lose time when I shower with You. But this isn't the forgetful veil of alien abduction shrouding my mind—it's divine intervention.

The water never grows cold because You are the fire that frightens away any chill. Your powers are beyond those of electricity and modern technology. You are my god, my lover, and I am Yours whenever and however You want me.

Your hands smooth their way across my body. You leave no part untouched. I am a sacred vessel for Your holy love. Mold me. Polish me. Let the energetic pressure of your fingertips create surface decorations. I beg you to gild my insides with the pure gold of Your love. You are always so eager for the first coupling. I raise my chin to the spray and await Your thrusts. My thighs are spread for You, beloved.

Enter me. Take what you need from me.

You raise me upon Your cock, a blessed impalement. You are in charge. I surrender control. I drown as You lift me and force me to slide against Your penis. Your thick head pushes into the vault of my womanhood. You are capable of hitting not only my G-spot, but every other letter in the alphabet and I'm sure some letters that are not remotely human. This first bout of shower coitus may be for You to feed or bring You release in order to slow things down, but it is my voice I hear in climax. You need only glance my way and my passion is quelled. Though truly, my beloved, I enjoy it so much more when my orgasm derives from every part of You melted into me in sexual union.

I hear Your pleasure fills the stall and ring out like pilgrims reaching holy ground, then soft laughter. I feel the final surge of Your orgasm. Hotter than the spray, it trickles out of me and sparkles like a thousand fireflies in the night.

You take a moment. I am pinioned upon You. You hold me close and coo. I don't understand what You are saying. I don't need to understand with my mind and logic, for the overwhelming feelings of love pulsing between us speaks volumes. I swear You speak in bird song as You come off the high of spilling inside me. Is there no language worthy of our love save for the call of a Chinese partridge?

Him

I am eager to take you again. Sometimes it's about sex. Sometimes it's about energy exchange. Sometimes I just need you like a man needs his supper. I am the inspiration for Hungry Man dinners. I am alive because of your love. I thrive because of your love. Without you, I am nothing but history—a memory, a story. You bring me into this world. I love you so dearly. What can I do for you, my beloved?

How can I help you enjoy your mundane life just a little more? Where should I touch you? What part of you shall I kiss first? I feel a part of you, which throbs against my shaft.

It beckons me to taste, suck, lick, and caress it. Your pink nub, your clitoris. A precious gem hidden in a great cave of riches that is your body—is your love. Allow me this honor, this privilege. I shall kneel before you. I will worship you and drink in your orgasm. I cherish your flavor. Your scent. I could endure another thousand years bound to jagged rocks at the ends of the Earth as long as your odor is on the breeze to caress me. Oh, sweet velvet. You are so soft. Your thighs are silken. Your labia is candy. It is at this moment—the moment I touch my tongue to your hot vulva—that I thank all the forces of the universe for making me a shape-shifter. As you shudder, I know you, too, are grateful.

Her

Your tongue should be packaged and sold as a shower massager. The hot pulse against my sensitive lady bits pulls me to a place beyond pleasure. I abandon thoughts of day job drama, low-balance checking accounts, flea meds for the dogs...I leave this realm when Your silver tongue speaks its sensual language against me—and in me.

Symbols pass before my eyes like a carnival carousel. You speak in code. Or perhaps it is that I hear You in a way my over-stimulated human mind can comprehend—in pretty pictures and colors. I have never cared to hazard a guess and interpret Your cryptic messages when You dole them out to me during sex. Do not speak to me now of serpents and mountaintops ringed by fire. How can I concentrate on lore and study or incantations while You perform cunnilingus? Oh, my beloved, You are indeed a trickster. If Your lessons were less veiled, would I still crave the sound of Your voice? It is the mystery that keeps me enthralled. With You, it is an eternal game of "The Lady or the Tiger." You create the problem and offer the solution simultaneously. I release myself to Your ministrations and pray that if the lessons You teach me as I climax against Your sweet face are valuable, that I will recall them.

Him

Delicious. You are precious, rare, and are the well-spring from which I rise. From your body flows the stuff of life. I drink in your orgasm as readily as you drink your morning coffee. You are my flesh, my blood, my bone, and soul. Your heart nourishes me. Each beat ebbs and flows in a tide of energy. I want to bear your children. I love you that dearly. I must create something magical from our love. I am not of this world, nor have I ever been. I am cosmos, universe, everything—male, female. I am Divine.

I put my hardness to your swollen labia and press inward. I want to spill inside you again and strike a spark of life. From this sacred communion of heat, water, and steam, let your strong humanity blossom within me. I am mother to many, father to many more. I am Husband, wife, and partner to all manner of creatures throughout the realms. But nothing can ever compare to the love I shall have for our child. Beautiful mortal woman...let me love you, worship you, be quickened by you. I am shaken and stirred and vivified as I come deep inside you. My seed, your ripe body—this is the stuff of magic.

I shall love our child born of heat and steam, whatever incarnation of spirit it takes from the mystic union of god and mortal. I love you. And I love shower time.

Loki-rotica III: The Receptive Mare
Darragha Foster

He knows my heart. He knows my desires, my needs, my fears. He knows every iota of me, and as my teacher, uses my own will and whims against me, and yet ultimately, for me. He is the harbinger of change. He is the flame that burns to bedrock, and the gentle wind that returns topsoil so young shoots may spring again from the earth. Some call him a devil. A trickster. A rascal. He is all those things. He is the sum of them, and He is more than them.

I heard His voice from a young age. I didn't understand the language he spoke for many years—at least not intellectually. To me, he was the rustling leaves in the trees, the flow of the tide over the shore, and the song of birds. He moved me to explore and push boundaries. I saw His shadow while picking berries during the summer and babysitting in the fall. I saw His form appear in the soapsuds of the dish water at my first real job. I saw His smile in the pancake syrup remains and burned edges of my hashbrowns at Sunday brunch. I didn't know His name at first. He was my secret. And together, from an early age, we wrote. And we rode.

The wind of heaven is that which blows between a horse's ears. He is my heaven. He was with me the moment I put riding boot to stirrup. He was the perfume caught in the torrents of divine breeze. I captured his scent on the trail, in the arena, and across open fields when I rode for the pure joy of riding—sans saddle, lead rope only. Upon dismount, I put pen to paper as my horse grazed and we wrote poetry. Poetry advanced in nature for my tender years. It was within those words I experienced my first kiss. His lips pressed to mine, tenderly. Eagerly. He came on the wind, swept me into His arms, and embraced me with such deep passion I swooned. Me, alone, under a tree in a field, kissed by fire and spirit. His kiss lingered for hours. And his touch tingled in parts of me just barely awakened. I touched myself for the first time that night. There was no other way to quell the passion blossomed within me. It made me desirous of a real paramour. I was ready for love and open to exploration. He said it would come in time. Until then, He was my muse, and I, His adoring pupil.

I was seventeen when I heard Him utter words—real words, not words of empathic measure, but audible, concise words. His English was broken and guttural. His voice was deep and rich—sexy. I was in the arms of that long-awaited boyfriend when first I heard Him. It was a simple request, or perhaps a warning. "Lay not with this boy." So, I didn't. I wanted to, but I chose to listen to my personal Jiminy Cricket, my spirit, my muse. On the eve of my eighteenth birthday, in meditation, He came to me. We made love for the first time. It was an astral loss of virginity to a spirituous being whose history was as rich and varied and as infinite as the heavens. I swear I walked bow-legged for a week after He took me on a pink cloud over a green valley. Or maybe it was a green cloud and a pink valley. All I know for certain is I was intact in the waking world and fucked hard Elsewhere. Meditation was never the same again.

I wondered why I had not lost my physical virginity to my first love for years—until I actually did. It was with a man I truly loved; a practiced man—not a boy in the backseat of a car. What really made the experience memorable was that my then-fiancé's smile changed as we made love. I saw the face of my muse—His smile, His incredibly delightful smile. I call moments such as those "pop-ins." For a few minutes, I was physically with Him. I can tell the difference between my husband's cock and His. I have never told my husband about my life-long companion. He is still my secret.

I was twenty-seven and married a year. I'd gone from writing poetry to experimental gender-fluid erotica under the pen name of Vesper Johns. I got paid by the word, just like the pulp writers of old. I had a following, a blog, a Pinterest board and did all the posts and tweets required of me by my publisher. And I had a muse and riding companion that inspired me to greatness. Until I told him I wanted to level up. Full-length novels. Movie scripts. No more day job.

That's when He brought out the lunge whip.

I'd taken up meditation so early in life I had developed an ability to trance deeply and soundly and remember everything. I look back now and realize I had taken Him a bit for granted. Although He'd never spoon-fed me a damned thing, He had certainly spoiled me. The real work was about to begin.

We met, as always, on a park bench somewhere in an astral realm.

"I want to write more than shorts. You're my muse. Muse me. Please."

"You're too hot," He said.

I knew the term. Any horsewoman would. "I am ready for more. Feed me."

"I have fed you all your life. I have nurtured and cared for you all your life. I have protected you. What you ask now is a thing that takes discipline beyond three thousand words a day. You're too hot. Too green. Too impatient."

I looked into His flame-filled brown eyes and demanded a new lesson. "Loki, I am ready."

I rarely addressed Him by his true name. Sure, I'd guessed His identity years prior. I wasn't blind to the signs and wonders that screamed Norse god. I chose to ignore them because He was my muse, and I was His author and lover and that was how I needed things to be in order to feel safe. No—to keep that status quo. To avoid rocking the boat. I never was big on change.

Then, the trickster turned me into a horse—a bay thoroughbred mare. My legs were taped, and attached to my halter was a damned stud chain and lunge rope. He held a long whip out before me. I had lunged my horse a hundred times, but I had never been on the pupil end of the rope before.

He clicked his tongue. "Walk on."

My rage that He felt I needed training at the end of a rope before musing me to another level of authordom knew no bounds. I held my ground.

"Walk on," He commanded.

I shook my long neck and kicked.

"Don't say no to me. Walk!"

He held the whip out toward my shoulder. He had a solid technique. I was not going to be able to ignore His commands and drag Him across the arena or buck at Him and get Him square in the jaw—though the thought appealed to me. I had the strength now. I had horsepower now—literally. I was a great ship; a fluid beast of equine perfection. No wonder heaven is found between my ears and across my poll. A horse is divinity on the hoof.

I had a twenty-foot lead and I proceeded to walk the circle. He rotated as I moved, the whip pointed at me.

"Trot."

I heard the command as my own horse would have heard it. The word had no meaning. The intention behind the word was everything. My ego would have had me lurch and balk at the command. The magnificent body I wore wanted only to obey and I trotted. Proud, I rounded my neck and gave Him a pretty pony, then I flicked my long tail and high-stepped.

He clicked for me to go faster. I nickered.

He pointed the lunge whip. "Steady, girl. Canter." He clicked again.

Fine! I'll show you what I can do. Lunging me this way is insulting, but I'll play along. Sure. I'll canter.

I rolled my shoulders forward, lowered my head, and took off. He immediately gave the command to "whoa."

I was pissed. I wanted to go—go fast.

"Ah, my pet, I see the fire in your eyes now. Remember, the purpose of lunging is to teach obedience and respect on the ground. For rider to build trust with the beast. Before you can fly, you must grow wings. How can you write when you lack discipline? How can I be muse to a gnat?"

I shook my large body and hoofed the ground.

He clicked and calmly, but forcefully, gave command. "Canter!" I took off.

On the end of a twenty-foot lead, Loki skillfully turned on a dime as I circled. Round after round. I broke a sweat. Freedom never tasted so sweet. Hoof to ground in unison. Perfection. I am a horse. I am a creature created by the gods. I am...aroused...

He gave the command to stop. I did so. I wanted him to ride me. Desperately. Ride me now. Across a field. Through a creek. Up a hill. In an arena. I don't care. *Mount me!*

"Hmmm. I see I have a receptive mare at my disposal. What shall I do?"

Ride me! I screamed it in every language. The oldest of languages.

Desire.

"I heard that."

There is a holy connection between horse and rider. And when the ride occurs on an astral plain, sparks fly. Loki didn't even command me to end the canter. He mounted mid-stride, the lunge rope slung over his shoulder. He had perfect form. I responded to the touch of His knees and gentle tug of His hand as if we had been riding for years. Well, horseback riding with me as His mount, at least.

With him astride, my hooves became flint to steel. Each step brought forth flame. The flames danced around my head, tickling nose and ears. Loki's gentle, but firm, precise, perfect equitation, urged me on.

We circled a great arena. Nothing mattered save our connection. Nothing. I anticipated His ride. He gave a non-verbal command to slow to a trot, then a walk. He uttered a deep, throaty "whoa." I stopped; my large horse heart raced. He rode me so hard. And I knew a harder ride was to come. I felt His longing for me.

With the grace and fluidity of a dancer, Loki shape-shifted from man to stallion—a magnificent, huge shire, dapple gray and proud, his member fully descended. He put his horse's nose to my rump and breathed in my scent.

Instinctively, I winked. That part of me ready to accept his sex pulsated and grew moist. I released pheromones to indicate my receptivity and flirted my tail against his long face. My human soul hidden in horsehair blushed at the sheer wantonness of the mare's body. *I am acting shamelessly. I want to rub my rump against Him. Mount me!*

He mounted me, all right. His size eclipsed me. I was no small pony at sixteen hands. He, however, was a shire, and easily nineteen hands. I let Him take me. I wanted His horse cock inside me. I backed into Him as He plunged. He wasn't booted. The bones of His legs tore at my coat. I wanted this. Pain or not. I wanted Him. I closed my horse eyes to feast on every sensation.

When I opened my eyes, I was again a woman.

I was on all fours. He was behind me, in me, fully male. All man. I heard His wicked cackle and caught a glimpse of His long red braid as He slid in and out of me.

He pulled away and rolled me. My legs were thrust up, knees to ears. He again pressed into me. He held my breasts and teased my clit with each pass.

We shared an orgasm—a long, deep, wet climax surrounded by sweet cedar shavings and the sounds of birds in the arena rafters.

I still wore the damned stud chain. Breathless, I pulled it off. "A shire? Really? I think You cracked my ribs. Is it some kind of godly preoccupation with size? On any mundane level mating a thoroughbred and shire would prove problematic. The product of such a pairing would be off-balance and an idiot."

He collapsed against me, still buried inside me. "You enjoyed every second. I love you, you know." His whisper reminded me of a warm breeze. "There will be no foal—or child—from this union, unless you wish it. Heaven is full of divine babies. Astral pregnancies are often much easier than earthly ones."

"I love You, too. But no ponies or babies, all right?"

"I do so love children. However, I know it is your wish to create not children of flesh, but children of written word. So, tell me, now that you've been worked and sweated and fucked, can you listen to me? Or do I need to put you on a donkey wheel?"

I smoothed away errant strands of hair from His perspiration-ridden forehead. "I'll listen."

"I love it when you are receptive to me. It's not so much that I must inspire you any differently, as it is you who must reach inside yourself and tap your reserves and resources. You are hot—and I don't mean that in the equine sense. Your writings are hot. Just keep doing what you're doing, and things will progress naturally. I can't just snap my fingers and hand you everything you want on a silver platter. Humanity ultimately rejects such things. You'd get bored."

"Sounds like work."

Loki's laugh echoed through me. "Work with a capital 'W', yes."

"I could be any of Your women. Is our answer always the same to whichever question we pose? Are You the great well of inspiration but not its catalyst?"

"I love the one I'm with, and I am certainly not muse to all."

"Are you not a god?"

"I am."

"Then why not just make it happen? I am ready." I slid out from under Him and sat upright.

He rose to face me, hunched upon His knees. His thick cock had not yet deflated. The red tendrils of pubic hair distracted me as He scolded me. "Oh, dear. Must I lunge and fuck you into a state of complete exhaustion every day until you realize I am not going to gift you a damned thing? Nothing is worth it unless you earn it for yourself."

"I'm afraid."

"Of writing? Of success? Of flying free? Puny mortal problems."

I dropped to my knees and slid into His arms. "Fuck you, you know?"

"Yes, I know. I'm a rascal."

"So, we shall see if my desire to be a successful novelist is stronger than my need to push out a ton of pulp-style fiction for the money. I'm not sure I will be taken seriously by mainstream publishers."

"Overcoming self-doubt and fear is a bitch, huh?"

"It's a puny mortal problem, yes. I've broken many horses of irrational fears. I could put you through paces while tossing hoses and balls at you. Would that help? Give you the boogey-monster treatment so you'll learn to be unafraid when something new challenges you? It works on my beloveds as well as horses, you know."

I shook my head. "I'm not sure that would help, at all. Are there other ways you can render assistance?"

Loki again reclined into the cedar chips. "Look, a horse is afraid of what it doesn't know or understand. It's afraid a shadow might eat it. You are afraid of what you don't know—and are afraid of the shadow of success. The wind of heaven, dear one—find it, embrace it, dance in it."

"The wind of heaven is that which I create."

"Yes," He said. "Now mount me."

I laughed and did just that, realizing that atop him, with him inside me—my muse inside me—my written words would conjure the wind of heaven.

Loki-rotica IV: That Old Time Religion
Darragha Foster

I walked upon newly turned rich, red earth, flanked by tall maples and strong evergreens, in almost utter darkness, lit only by the light of my cell phone and the fabulous Milky Way above. There was a titillating bite in the air. An aura of Spirit and mystical energy flowed along the path, whipping in between my feet like a playful miniature dachshund. It tickled all parts of me. I gave it consent. I offered it thanks. It touched me intimately and smiled as slyly at me as does the Trickster at play. I walked on, the embrace of a god still with me. Always with me. — excerpt, *A Walk Across the Vault of Heaven* by Verity Thompson.

Who is Loki? He is the Norse god of mischief. Trickster. Harbinger of life-altering change. Frequent lover of mortals, by way of human vessel or astral encounter. His touch is healing. Healing like the debridement of flesh to clean dead and contaminated material from a wound to aid in healing. Painful, yet necessary. He is a walk-through flame, a hard ride, and yet, a compassionate, patient deity dedicated to both laughter and sorrow. To Work with Loki is to invite a swell of chaos into your life. Chaos with heart, heat, poetry, inspiration, and freedom at its core. When Loki asks you to dance with him, be prepared to teeter on the edge and fall into darkness only to see that when you arise, it was your own hand that lifted you.

Chapter One

Verity Thompson took stock of the faces of her class before speaking. They looked ready. Alert. Interested. Thank gods. She needed these students to enjoy her lessons so much they would petition for a follow-up section. She straightened the hem of her sweater and took a breath. She pointed to the whiteboard where she'd written the class number and title. Confidently, she addressed the students.

"Sacred sexuality is a thing. Hanging out with Hellenics or Lokeans or those who practice Santeria—there's always a couple of priests or priestesses willing to draw down a god or spirit, and in the "gift for a gift" mode, perform acts of a sacred sexual and/or intimate nature. This is the epitome of what could be called *that old-time religion*. Sacred sex goes back to the Neolithic Mother cults, and it is alive and well to this day. Although it is hush hush now because so many people are influenced by Puritanical mores, and so many believe that any act of sensuality cannot have anything to do with spirituality. Sensationalism precedes sacred sex with fear that all children are at risk of being molested by Satanists and that pedophiles are all heathen. In fact, the spirits I work with would go ballistic if a child was put in harm's way. Sacred sexuality is not fluffy, bunny, unicorn fart, pseudo, witchy paganism.

Sacred consorts, holy whores—male, female or otherkin—are usually powerful channels, open to Spirit, and without the belief system instilled in them that sex is bad. Rituals are done in sacred space, and if intimate contact is negotiated, safe sex is practiced. Sometimes there is no physical embrace of passionate nature. Sometimes it's a slow fuck against the fridge, 'cause the sacred space extends into the kitchen and that's where the participants ended up. Sometimes the vessel hosting the god, goddess, or spirit remembers the whole shebang. Sometimes bits and pieces. Sometimes *nada*. Sometimes it's just the full body giggle of a stellar orgasm as one rushes to put clothes back on, the only audible sound being the words, *What the fuck just happened?"*

A student about four rows back raised her hand.

"Yes?"

"Ms. Thompson – are you shitting us?"

Verity Thompson, community college instructor and life-time pagan, laughed. "No. The title of this course is *Sacred Sex in the Modern Era*. It is a fully vetted class. Did you read the syllabus? There is no shitting of anyone here. Now, sacred sex can take many forms. From eco-sexual encounters to those I mentioned and will mention. Why, in some traditions the union of husband and wife is considered sacred." She shook her head. "Good thing this is a ten-week course. We have lots of ground to cover, including getting a few of you to move beyond a state of disbelief."

"Will our final test be an orgy?" another student asked.

"No. At least not one of which I will play any part. I anticipated this comment and want you all to put your lesser brains on hold. Sacred sexuality is not about orgies and free sex.

It is about honoring the gods and giving them an opportunity to use a human host to honor their people in return. As for an orgy...what you do on your own time is your affair. I recommend, however, that you only fly with an experienced witch. Meaning, do not *horse* without understanding the nature of *Gebo*."

The class' stunned faces and simultaneous mouthing of the word, "horse," almost caused Verity to bust a gut. She took a deep breath and maintained composure. "Which term do you want defined first? *Gebo* or *horse*? Never mind. Let me continue today's lecture and we will touch upon both topics."

Like automatons, the twenty-three students in the class nodded in unison.

"A gift for a gift—or Gebo—is the basis for most encounters. We are working with the premise here that the old gods—and new spirits such as those found in pop culture paganism, and other spirits of land, sea, and sky—or even treadmills, toasters, and sex toys, are real, and are sometimes quite interested in a little quid pro quo. The belief in many gods is called Polytheism. Loki, of Norse Mythology, not the Marvel comics/Disney Loki, is one such god with great interest in playing a little game of *this for that*. Modern worshippers of this fascinating Norse god are, in many cases, able to draw out his energy and make the rituals they hold the best parties ever." Verity waited for the class to finish their giggles and nervous twitters. "There are many levels of ritual. From lighting a candle and invoking a god by name to more elaborate ceremonies involving costumes, mead, and quarter calls. It really depends on time, place, circumstances, and what you and the god or spirit wants—and what you have to offer and what you want in return."

"What could a god possibly want? Are they not powerful in their own right? So much so that they can..."

Verity held up her hand to hold the student's question. "The gods—at least the Norse gods—adhere to and rely on the rules of hospitality. They generally respect freewill and wait to be invited. I know of only a few instances wherein Loki or Odin has muscled their way into a host. Truly, when that happens, it never ends well for either party. You know the lore about how vampires need to be invited into a house before they can whip up a light snack? Same thing with the gods. At least this is true for the ones I discuss in this course. I'm sure there are spirits and gods that usurp and control—but that is not germane at present time. The Norse gods, such as Loki, and gods of the Orisha, use hosts to interact and communicate with worshippers. Both belief systems use the term "horse" for the act of connectedness between mortal and spirit. The god "rides" the mortal, and based on pre-set terms—a contract—the mortal moves in society. Basically, you get a walking, talking, sometimes fucking, Loki. And Loki, who is gender fluid, does not hesitate to horse a person of either sex, or even a non-binary individual. I have interviewed horses—vessels—who were straight, but willing to allow Loki to make love to a worshipper who was of the same sex. Not because the vessel was bi-curious, but because their contract with Loki specified such things. Another vessel allowed integration for what I might call a "Norse Mythology Passion Play" where attendees were invited to interact with a half-dozen gods at a festival with lore retellings and food. I understand that Loki once horsed a chef because he likes to cook. Just cook. In the case of the sacred sexual acts I have investigated, the host wanted divine inspiration to achieve a goal or solve a problem, and the god wanted to interact physically with a devotee because of love or reward. Yes, the gods love. Some even have mortal husbands or wives. Or both. People have and do dedicate themselves to the gods—just as nuns are the brides of Christ. And yes, they, the gods, grant boons. Sometimes a god or spirit wants to impart healing through the laying on of hands. I'd say that sometimes they impart wisdom, but in Loki's case, not so much. He is the Trickster, and his wisdom is oft times garbled or covert. Moreover, the host must interpret the words, thoughts, and deeds of the god—and it has been reported that sometimes there are no words to describe Loki's wishes. No human words, at least. Did I answer your question?" She nodded to the student who had raised her hand. The young woman gave her a thumbs-up. Verity continued, "Any questions before I move on to contracts and levels of trust?"

The adult students let out a collective exhale.

Verity smiled inwardly. *Eating it up. I am so going to get asked back to teach another session.*

A student in the back of the room stood. "Is there a verification process? I mean, you wouldn't want your ritual contaminated by a fake horse."

"Yes. Passwords. I've discovered that many worshippers are already in communication with their gods to varying degrees, and some have passwords set up should there be a physical communion. It is prudent to develop such barriers to horsing. The gods will also bless a medium with a vision of which only the worshipper is aware to solidify the purity of the encounter. I can share an example here. A medium, a very god-touched young woman, told a worshipper that she'd had a vision of said worshipper's past life. The worshipper had been told of this lifetime before—twenty years' prior in another state by another psychic but had never mentioned it to anyone—least of whom, the new medium. The medium went on to channel Loki, and eventually horse Loki, for the worshipper and a small coven. Good times."

"This is complex," a student replied.

"Indeed. From consent to grounding, sacred sexuality is a healthy, but complex, ritual. Oh, hey. See you Tuesday. Time's up. Read the text through chapter two. Drive home carefully now."

Verity turned to gather her notes as the class shuffled out. Her stomach growled. It was nearly seven in the evening, but she wanted a cup of coffee. Her mind on a sandwich and latte, she didn't notice a single student remained.

"I enjoyed your lecture," he said quietly.

She turned and pursed her lips. *I don't recall him being in the class.* "Thanks." Her stomach growled. "I'm sorry. I've got to close up now." Her pulse raced. She could feel the heat coming off this guy ten paces away. The root of her womanhood twitched. *Oh, dear gods...he is so affecting. Who is he? He is attractive. Holy Freyja, he has serious blue eyes.* She found herself repeating her initial question. *Who is he? He kind of looks like my sister's boyfriend—at least from the photos of him on her social media account. But it couldn't be him. He doesn't even live in the same state as her. Or me. But still...he does bare a strong resemblance to him.*

He rose from his chair, and carefully pushed it in. "I alarm you. How interesting."

Verity approached while dressing him down with her eyes. He couldn't have been more than six feet tall, but so perfectly proportioned that he was truly a thing of beauty to behold. Perfect. *This man is fucking perfect.* He turned sideways to avoid running into a student desk. Verity forgot to breathe. His jeans fit in all the right places, too. Just as some men preferred breasts or legs, she liked crotches. Some woman like butts or abs. It was all about the bulge for her. His devilish good looks and aura of sensuality enveloped her like a hurricane. *How could I have not noticed him in class?* "You don't alarm me. Now, if you don't mind, I'd like to head home."

"After a swing by that coffee shop that makes those killer sandwiches?"

"How did you know that?" She studied his face. She tasted chocolate on her lips. A telltale sign of spirit activity. Of Lokean activity. "Are you human?"

The man leaned forward and whispered a single word to Verity. "Jack London."

His words fell like a kiss against her face. *Words, like touch, can be so arousing.* They caressed and electrified her. She breathed in the heady aroma of his maleness and closed her eyes for a moment. Only for a moment. Beyond the veil of closed lids, she found herself drawn into a deep embrace with scarred lips she knew well. She spoke his name against his mouth. "Loki."

He replied softly, barely pulling away. "I am here, beloved. Hold me. Whisper your desires into my ear."

Verity giggled. "I don't know where to begin with that one. And I'm not sure this is the right place or time."

It didn't matter. He poured into her arms. No force in heaven or on earth could stop her from whispering her desires into his ear. The desires that only he brought out in her. She put lips to ear. "I want this class to be so well received the college hires me full-time and that they give me an entire AA degree course to teach in religious studies."

"Is that all?" he asked. "I had expected something a little naughtier."

"I want to lick my cum from your bearded chin."

Loki laughed as only he could. It sounded as sweet as church bells yet had the heat of a forge. He paraphrased a movie quote. "Verity calls for aid, and Loki will answer."

Verity stifled a snort of laughter to reply. "My beacon is lit. And yes, I get the vicarious *Lord of the Rings* quote.

"I got a million of them. Every movie, every book—anything artistic that one of my people have consumed, I have partaken of same."

"Hmmm. We'll have to play Trivia Pursuit ™ sometime. But not right now."

"No, not right now." He entered her as only a divine shape-shifter could. Not a phallus of flesh, but one of energy. She beheld the stranger's face—the face of her sister's boyfriend. She felt his weight atop her. In her. The pure rush of climax surged through her. He took what he needed, and in return, gave her so much more than she could ever ask. It wasn't Loki's usual fire-brown eyes she saw in the darkness as the exchange ended. The eyes smiling at her were blue. Bright blue. Smart ass blue.

Verity shook herself out of the vision. First glance went to the clock. The entire encounter took only a few moments. But in magical haze of those few seconds, Loki had pleasured her, inspired her, and aroused determination in her, then vanished. She stood, head cocked to one side, at the doorway to the portable that acted as her classroom. *Jack London. Then poof! What the fuck?* She locked the door behind her and headed to her car. *Jack London. My favorite author. My password. My password should I ever experience physical communion with a god.* She thumbed through her class list on her phone. Each student's ID card photo was listed by his or her name. He didn't exist. A handsome face with deep set, brilliant blue eyes. Salt and pepper hair. Sweet goatee that she thought perhaps, in hindsight, she might, indeed, wish to lick. *An iteration of her sister's lover. He certainly is a handsome devil. Chari picked herself a looker. Why choose that appearance, Loki?*

Verity was too hungry and needed caffeine too desperately to freak out over having her patron bless her with a conjugal visit in an astral body strongly resembling the few social media photos she'd seen of her sister's boyfriend. She felt her blood sugar dropping rapidly and blood pressure rising from the sensuality of the moment. It wasn't her first time at the rodeo. They mashed together in dreams or meditations, in varying degrees, on a frequent basis. It was part of the package when you worked with Loki. She'd seen Loki use vessels. He'd just never given her undivided attention in-body before. In fact, at the rituals she'd attended where a human drew down Loki's spirit, she'd barely been noticed. This wasn't exactly that—but close enough to make her *Spidey senses* tingle. *He hadn't been physical. It simply appeared that way. It wasn't a horse. It wasn't a channel. It wasn't a wight. It wasn't he wasn't here. But why choose the unfamiliar appearance? Do I harbor an unspoken attraction to my sister's boyfriend? Not that I am aware.* Spirit work was both rewarding and frightening. A great and terrible thing. *And now I'm teaching a class chock full of spirit-talk. No wonder the gods are afoot.* She patted the hex bag hanging off her rearview mirror. It provided a level of protection more in a traditional sense than a literal one—but it made her feel safe. Not that she feared the Trickster. In meditation and dreams, she had discussed the advent of being loved on by him in a meat suit. In human form. Using a human to enact his wishes on a mortal plain. Or even just having lunch. It wasn't always about sex. *All right—Loki is all about sex, even when it's not sex. It is the energy exchange and gift for a gift he craves. He said the password.* What does that mean?

Her cell phone chirped. She pushed the button on her Bluetooth headset. "Talk to me."

"Verity. I have good news." It was her twin sister, Charity. "I got the loan. We are going to own a fabulous old, converted hotel with a restaurant on the main floor and a huge meeting space upstairs. Huge. Someone—a long time ago—opened up the second-floor rooms to make one grand room. There were originally a dozen sleeping quarters—from a master suite to a room with a sink and bunkbeds. There are bathrooms with old-fashioned clawfoot tubs on either end. And best of all, the great room has a chandelier. The most beautiful antique lighting I've ever seen. It once graced the foyer downstairs, which is now restaurant seating. It has an old brass elevator and almost all the original fixtures. Best of all—previous owners updated and wiring and plumbing. All I need to do is repair some plaster and rip out some god-awful carpeting. There's hardwood under it. I have about twenty days to come up with the money I need to pay at closing, which isn't included in the loan. And because this is commercial property, it's painful. But we can do this. Johnny and me. We are going to come together and make our dreams happen."

"That's great news. It isn't an old bordello, is it?"

Chari laughed. "Maybe."

"I like that energy. What fun. You and your mystery man got it all worked out, then." It was more a statement than a question.

"He's not a mystery. You just haven't met him yet."

"He's been your boyfriend for over a year. And I haven't met him." *Do I tell her about Loki appearing in his form?*

"Well, that's going to change. He's moving to the area, and I tell you…he looks fine in chef's whites."

"How much do you need at closing?"

"A major fuck ton. I got the property and buildings for six hundred thousand. I put my entire inheritance into it, and Johnny cleaned out his savings. But, this is what we want."

"Going to have that room you always wanted to hold rituals?"

"Upstairs. Yes. And on the grounds. There's a meadow completely surrounded by maple trees. The trees are concentric. The meadow was created to be out of sight of the main building. It's like a big fairy circle. There's a little caretaker shack, too. It is too sweet. I've already applied for the 501C3. Revived Intimacy, LLC." Chari paused. "Best of all, there is an old bunkhouse on the grounds that can be rented out to groups of less than a hundred. I think I counted at least that many berths. I'll need to do some updating there—get new futons and lighting. Maybe put in a patio and brick oven. That can come later. There are shower stalls and a wooden walkway that leads to the bay. I am so stoked."

Verity laughed. "Am I on the Board? VP?"

"Yes."

"Well, your patrons can enjoy a good meal then go 'round the back and upstairs for a little old-time religion. A sacred sexual tent revival. Alleluia, and pass the prophylactics."

"Seriously old timey, yes. I'll be utilizing traditions from across the globe for circle."

"I started teaching my class on sacred sexuality this evening." Verity yawned. "I am beat, sis."

Charity giggled. "Well, I hope I can give you enough fodder to teach another course. Practical application, since you have been so very academic and theoretical regarding all the things, forever. You're heading home?"

"You'll have to be careful about how the ritual is advertised and/or shared. Anyone participating must be vetted and sign a non-disclosure agreement. And you won't have to worry about the care and feeding of your horses and other participants. You can just ring down for a snack."

"The building is outside the city limits, but accessible, with a tree-lined driveway with Agate Bay on one side. I won't schedule sky-clad rituals during dinner service." Charity laughed. "Not every ritual will involve the sharing of body parts. It depends upon the attendees, spirits, and gods who care to participate. I can't imagine Artemis desiring sacred touch. Now, *your* Norse gods, yes. I can't think of any that wouldn't enjoy a bit of consensual play. I'm going to hire a caretaker to hold space. Keep the spirits in check. I feel the need to have twenty-four-hour prayer for a bit. A stop-gap for rogue draw downs. You'll visit, won't you? Join in a ritual as a participant, not just an observer? My sister, who experiences sacred sex second hand."

"Unless it's my patron calling me to my knees I'm not interested in participation. And I'm in no hurry to have a physical relationship with a god."

Charity sighed. "You, my sweet, are a liar. I'm sure you harbor secret desires to take on a horse—male or female." She paused. "Johnny has a relationship with Loki. Did I tell you that?"

"You did not." *Why are you telling me this now?* "And I think I'd like a male horse. Loki knows that. Gods, and not one of those movie Loki cosplayers. I want a mature man, not a kid still wet behind the ears."

"He's aspected Loki before. And even led some rituals of a more Lokean nature. And don't knock cosplayers—to some it is a divine offering of their time and energy."

I am totally not surprised. "A chef and a Loki's man. What more could you ask? And I apologize to all cosplayers. Far be it for me to disdain anyone's form of worship."

"Sis, I need to make something clear. I know you. And I do not offer it to me. I know you. I don't want your money. This is my labor and I trust the universe to show me the way to earn the funds. The gods have directed me to draw fortune to myself from ten thousand miles afar. So far, I've had all the money needed to get this going."

Verity laughed. "Money is a piece of cake for Loki. Maybe have your old man do a little invocation. Loki responds well to cookies. Snickerdoodles. He loves them. And just because you are a few minutes older doesn't mean you can tell me what to do. If I want to help you, I will."

"Hmm. Well, Johnny did say on the phone the other day that he'd sell anything to get the restaurant. That gives me an idea. But maybe making cookies would suffice."

"Johnny shouldn't be so general when working with Loki. *Anything* could mean *anything*. It's best to be quite specific with a trickster. You know what I mean? Hey, I'm driving. Chat later?" *My gut tells me I don't want to know what your idea is.*

"Love you, sis. Later!" Charity replied.

The silence of the road was in sharp contrast to the din of the classroom and then short but animated conversation with her sister. Drive time was sometimes the only personal time she had during the day. Especially on days she taught several sections. Not to a point of distraction, but sometimes her patrons did message her during the quiet of the twenty-minute commute home. Loki turned her hazard lights on randomly. Or she heard him laughing. He was the epitome of "gotta be a pony in here somewhere." She planned on using that story as a talking point in the sacred sex class. When life appeared to be handing you a big pile of manure, look closer. *Gotta be a pony in there somewhere.* That is life with Loki.

She had to stop at a railroad crossing. Verity closed her eyes as the whir and clack of heavy steel broke the silence in rhythm to the tune wafting about her brain. In between the boxcars she could see the bright sign of her drive-thru ahead. A beacon of hope. Coffee. Food. She rifled around in her bag for a piece of hard candy. Something needed to go into her mouth now or there would be a major scarfing of all available foods. Not only would she order and consume a whole sandwich, but coffee, a shake, and a cookie, too. Best to stave off the hunger. As soon as the peppermint flavor touched her tongue, she realized it was not that kind of hunger. *I am experiencing the pangs of wantonness. Sweet. Thanks for that, Loki. It will certainly make my solitary pleasure more interesting this evening.* She lifted her foot off the brake in preparation to pull forward as the last boxcar sped past. "Of course, I'm open to a mortal relationship, Loki. Fantasies, dreams, and visions aside, I could use a good *rogering* from someone a little less ethereal. Maybe a bonded, committed relationship with an articulate, intelligent, patient man. Someone to come home to after a long day's work." Who am I kidding? I am not in a position to meet potential partners. Too shy, too jaded, too busy.

She heard a low throaty chuckle. *Yep. He's listening.*

Verity slid into the drive-thru and then put her car in Park. She tapped her finger against the steering wheel as she waited for the clown face to acknowledge her. She called all drive-thru speakers "clown face." This one did not have a face, not even a screen. Just a speaker. She didn't want to wait for the formalities and niceties of communicating with the teenager behind the screen. "I want a turkey on rye with swiss, no mustard or lettuce and extra onion. And a twenty-ounce latte. Please."

"A turkey and swiss on rye, no mustard or lettuce, extra onion, and a twenty-ounce latte. Will that be all?"

She had to smile at the young voice wafting through the speaker. He was trying so hard. "Yes, thank you."

"We'll have your total at the window. Please pull forward."

"Thank you." She shifted out of Park and depressed the gas. Her hazard lights came on. "What the... Loki!"

She turned off the flashers and unrolled her window to pass her debit card through to the clerk.

Her hazard lights flipped on a second time. She closed her eyes, hoping to hear the message—feel the message—in the brief span of time between paying and the deployment of coffee down her gullet.

All she saw, as if sitting in a dark theater watching images on a movie screen, was the cover of *Call of the Wild*. She sent a mental message to her patron. *What are you plotting, Loki?*

The cover of the Jack London short story, *To Build a Fire*, appeared behind her closed eyes.

"Here's your card, ma'am."

Vision interruptus. Message received, nevertheless. Jack London. The password to glory. I may be in for the ride of my life. But first, coffee. The poor minimum-wage working teen kept the smile frozen on his pasty face and arm extended with her card. She *could* just make him wait a moment longer before she retrieved the card to be mean. Not really her style. Well, before coffee...maybe.

She took the card and coffee, then the bag containing her food. It was hard to reply politely. Too hungry. Too desperate for coffee. "Thank you."

Cup balanced between her legs she put the car in Drive and then pulled into a parking spot in the back of the lot. She blew into the hole of her to-go cup to cool it a little. "All hail the goddess Caffeina, may her dark blessings energize me." A religious devotion, she tipped the cup so the hot, milky liquid reached her lips. That first taste. The whole-body anticipation.

The sensation of a well-brewed cup of Joe against her throat. The delicate aftertaste and smooth mouth-feel. Coffee. *Gods bless coffee.* This must be how vampires feel after their first feed. The pain ends. The blood is the life. Coffee is life. She took a longer sip. It burned a little. Sweet pain. Pain worth bearing. That subtle sting on her lips would remind her of the rapture of the embrace of the goddess. The proper devotion and consumption of coffee reminded her of a Bible verse she'd learned in a comparative religions class—*He will wipe away every tear from their eyes, and death shall be no more, neither shall there be mourning, nor crying, nor pain anymore, for the former things have passed away.* It's about Heaven. Coffee is heaven. Or at least, heavenly.

A few sips and satiation always set in. She'd forgotten to eat when in a rapturous state with Mr. Coffee. Good times. She took another sip. She didn't have anything pressing to do at home. And this parking lot was as good as any place to scroll through her social media feed and email. "Ah, the beauty of a car with built-in Wifi, a smart phone, and cup of Joe. I could die happy."

She opened the social media app and found she had a new friend request. She nearly choked on her latte when she saw the face of the requestor. It was the vanishing dude from class. *Jack London.* Johnny. Johnny Lightman. Her sister's beau and restauranteur. She accepted the request. *I believe in signs and wonders. This is being god-touched at its best. My sister's boyfriend is the face of he who knoweth my password for divine encounters. I am so screwed. Or maybe I'm going to be.* "Well, if I think about this while driving I will most certainly go off the road. Distract!" She turned on the radio—loud. *Drown out today's freaky-deaky paranormal occurrences. I kind of assumed that teaching a course on sacred sexuality would bring out the things that go bump and grind in the night. But this is rather unexpected.*

Charity had sent her a text. *Apparently, sis is in a bit of a freak-out over the money needed at closing.* Verity set her phone aside and pulled out, toward home. *I would really like to just give her the money she needs. I have it. I have yet to spend my inheritance. But I am also aware that her gods wish her to be self-sufficient in this undertaking. She's always wanted the sacred space, and with the addition of the restaurant, she should be able to make a go of things. She'll be fine. Don't freak out, Chari. Don't freak out. All those spirits and deities you honor got your back.*

Chapter Two

Home was a 1912 converted carriage house. It sat on the back side of a building lot where once had stood a grand mansion. Burned. Gone. Her stone, gothic-style home had two main rooms and a privy and kitchenette. The front door had been carved into the old solid oak entrance on the side used for the master's horses. The second oaken arched wall had been fitted with windows. It was unique. She polished the oak from floor to ceiling every few months. She'd ripped out the linoleum and torn down the dry wall. It took months of hard work, but the original stone walls and floors looked new. A couple of scatter rugs covered the areas that still needed a bit of work. She'd refitted the fixtures with period pieces but had just barely scratched the grounds. Yes. Grounds. Acres of land, both marshy and wooded, with an orchard and greenhouse. She and Chari had discussed building and developing *Reviving Intimacy* there. Way too costly. There were no utility connections or other infrastructure past the carriage house. It was also too far away. Chari had made a home for herself five hours south. Verity liked where she was. Liked her job. Loved teaching. The coffee was better up north. That kind of cinched it for her.

She ate mechanically. She truly needed to set aside the late evening coffee cravings. It might be more fun to fall asleep quickly and soundly since Loki was afoot. He was the epitome of *a good time*. Theirs was a pleasant relationship. They made love in dreamland and in meditations, and like today, she recognized him in her mundane world. *I am the blood hound to his fox. I always know when he's around.*

Bad habits die hard. Hoping to read herself to sleep, she climbed into bed and lit up the Kindle™ app on her phone. She read non-fiction for the most part. The half-hour before sleep hit was generally the only time of day she had to indulge in reading for pleasure. She thought audiobooks might be in her future, but she hadn't taken that step yet. Until then, it was the unhealthy glow of her phone's screen to illuminate her reads. She set her alarm and then plugged the cell into its long charging cord. She'd fallen asleep more than once, her only bed partner, her cell. Maybe it was time to get a cat.

Sleep came easily. She set things up that way. The blanket was very soft. The air temperature of the room just above chilled. A window opened a crack for air flow. A single soft pink light on above the stove that illuminated just enough of the corridor between bedroom and kitchen to make her feel safe. Bedroom door, ajar. Closet door, latched.

And happily, Loki was waiting.

Although one might believe the Norse god of chaos and change would trample traditions and ritual for a more loosey-goosey approach to mortal/god relations, this was not the case. Loki and Verity always met on a park bench, along a path leading into a forest. Then, they danced. Ballroom, Bollywood-style, a classic "stroll." He'd even had her square dancing once. Dancing was his metaphor for teaching, for learning. For life. Sometimes they danced their way through the forest to a cottage in a grove. Sometimes they danced into the ethers and otherworlds. This time, they just sat on the bench, holding hands, like an old married couple.

"Hello, beloved," he whispered.

Verity clutched his hand tightly. "Hello, Loki."

"I've not much time tonight. You know me, the god of change, always hopping." He kissed her temple.

"Was it you, today? Jack London?"

"Of course it was I."

"Is there something you'd like me to do, Loki?"

"I want you to offer your sister all the money she needs in an exchange."

Verity raised an eyebrow suspiciously. "Exchange for what?"

"A night with Johnny."

"Her boyfriend?"

Loki nodded. "I want you to offer her the money. In exchange, you and Johnny will enjoy sexual congress in a most sacred fashion. I'll take you and he having sex in the front seat of his truck if that's how things pan out. Just do me the honor of screaming out my name when you come."

"Loki, honey...that is..."

"Yeah, yeah, yeah. A matter of freewill. Whatever. Make the offer."

"It's *my* money, Loki. And my vagina. And Johnny's cock and..." She paused. "I don't know him. What if he doesn't want me?"

Loki kissed her temple again. "Don't listen to your little negative voice. He's a man, and though a man of morals and commitment, he is also a spiritual priest who will engage you in sacred rites in my name and, as you teach your students—for the *gebo*. He gets it. Just be patient until he's ready. For a man who can produce thirty covers of fine, quality dining in two hours when pressed, he certainly does become entrenched when under stress. He does not give up an iota of control under any circumstance. It will take a bit of cleverness on my part to get him to relax a little. I'll see you soon. Make the offer. I'll leave you with something to help you make your decision."

And he was gone.

Verity shook her head as Loki went poof! She found herself in her bed—though she could tell she was in a dream state.

A frantic knock on her door sent her to her feet. The floor was cold. A fine mist hung over her path to the living room. Dream fog. She blew it aside. She didn't want to pull any of it out of dreamland with her. Brain fog. Not cool upon waking.

The door opened on its own. On the other side stood Johnny Lightman, with a look of dire panic on his face. "He wants in! He won't leave me alone until I let him in."

"All right. Let him speak," Verity replied.

Loki jumped into Johnny—but there were no words spoken. He took Verity into his arms and kissed her long and deep. They made love as one can only in dreamland. Electric. Frenzied. Passionate.

She awoke, phone in hand, dried drool on the pillow side of her face and a bladder screaming for release. She rolled over and rose. "Oh, gods...I just got seriously laid in the astral."

It was just after midnight.

After relieving herself and forgoing coffee for a sip of water, Verity crawled back into bed. She texted her sister. *I just* *dreamed that I gave you $ to sleep with Johnny.* She chastised herself. *She is going to think I'm crazy.*

Took about thirty seconds to receive a reply. *He did say he'd sell anything to get the restaurant. We figured antiques, not his body. I'm not opposed to it.* There was an unusual pause, then shouting. All caps. *VERITY! HE COULD DRAW DOWN LOKI AND* (all caps off), *I could set a ritual up and make it all done in sacred space. You could donate to the 501C3, and we can both write off the closing costs. That is a total win/win. You've always wanted to have Loki in-body.*

Verity stared at her phone. There had to be more coming. Chari always spilled her guts—even in a text.

You can finally get a taste of sacred sexuality firsthand. Oh, and Loki put you up to this, didn't he?

Verity placed her cell to her forehead for a moment. *Oh, dear gods.* She typed a one-word reply. *Yes.*

Chari replied. *Well, then this will have to be a night worth remembering. Serious bang for serious buck. I know Johnny has it in him. I'm sure Loki does, too. But I have to tell you, I do have a line on the money. My 401k, the aforementioned antiques, and calling in a few favors. Johnny may not be willing, too. He has yet to engage in sacred sex as a priestly vessel, even though he has drawn down Loki a time or two. Just tossing out the caveat.*

Verity, as always, felt floored by her sister's ability to speak in full, grammatically correct sentences in a text message. She decided against sharing the vision of Johnny. She assumed her sister knew they were online friends now. *K. Get back to me. You know I'd give you the money if you asked, yes?*

Charity replied. *I'd never ask. I know how you like your money.* {smiley face}

Verity reclined and set her phone aside. "Hail Loki."
She heard him chuckle.

Chapter Three

Chari gave some thought to how she would approach Johnny. She'd learned to tone it down a bit when she was far too excited for her own good. He was a stoic man, having learned to be non-reactive while working as a police officer. He had deep spiritual insight, but rarely fed that flame. She knew that he worshipped with each dash of salt he tossed into a pan. Cooking was his communion, and a kitchen, his church. Every now and then he participated in a ritual, but mostly he cooked for them. He liked to be behind-the-scenes. Away from the crowd. She texted him. *Near your computer? Can I call?*

Sure. A one-word reply. *That's my Johnny.*

She depressed the telephone icon on her email's sidebar, and moments later, she and Johnny were connected. "Hey, babe."

"Hey, Chari."

"Verity and I kind of came up with an idea that would benefit all three of us."

"I'm afraid to ask what that idea is."

"It would mean not having to beg, borrow, or steal."

Johnny smirked. "That's a plus."

"I proposed to Verity that you draw down Loki."

"Why would that help?"

Charity could sense the tension in Johnny's voice. Better get right to the point. "She is steeped in non-experiential knowledge of sacred sex. You know this, right? Well, I figured it was time for her to get her feet wet."

"I'm afraid to ask, but what else will I help her get wet?"

"Johnny, would you draw down Loki and make love to Verity? She needs to understand the process in far less academic sense—and she will gift the LLC funds needed in return."

He laughed. "Gift for a gift."

"Yes." Chari paused. "Are you breathing? Johnny...say something."

"I had not considered sexual acts a part of my spiritual path. Give me a moment."

"Verity and I refer to this stuff as old- time religion." She paused. "That's a joke, honey."

"Very funny. I love you, Chari. I mean that. But this is a bit over the top. Even for you. It would certainly, if nothing else, further my experience into priesthood."

"And you did say you'd sell anything to get the property."

"Yes. Yes, I did."

"Is that a maybe?"

"Yes. It's a maybe."

Chapter Four

The daily grind continued. For Verity, literally. Her pre-programmed coffeemaker ground and brewed on a tight morning schedule. The coffeemaker cost more than her first car. She awakened every morning to what could only be described as the perfumed air of the gods.

The worship of Caffeina, a shower, morning devotions, ten minutes of local news, more coffee, some kind of portable protein for breakfast, and out the door, hopefully fully clothed with two earrings and one brooch or necklace and eyeliner, deployed. Two morning classes, then a break until three o'clock. Two more classes, then her night class. A full day of teaching. She realized as she pulled away that she'd forgotten to pack a lunch. Again. The cafeteria had okay food, but bad coffee. And no time to pick anything up on the way. *Damn. Community college cafeteria time.*

Comparative Religions 1 and 2. A breeze. Easy classes. Attentive students. She'd taught the courses for so many years she could do them by rote. It had been difficult to follow her own "no cell phone usage" in class rule when hers vibrated. As soon as her morning session ended she checked her messages.

And...nothing. She'd forgotten about the auto-draws from checking. The credit union pinged her balance updates. So far, her foray into sacred sex was all observation and firsthand accounts. Sis had not yet proclaimed that the love of her life had agreed to prostitute himself for closing costs. She pushed a tray along the rail of the cafeteria, hoping to find less-than-institutionalized foods for lunch. Sacred sexuality was not prostitution, per se. Devotees did make donations to the temple, priest or priestess calling the ritual, both in the past, where holy whores and sacred concubines were commonplace, to modern times wherein the rent had to be paid.

Mindless scoop of scrambled eggs went onto her plate. Salsa. Sautéed mushrooms. A small but probably satisfying lunch. She took a side of bacon. *Loki likes bacon*. It was a favorite offering.

It was time to let the situation rattle around her brain as she ate and pretended to read. She wasn't in the mood to share idle prattle with other staff or grad students. She wanted to make a list. She had been trying to wean herself off the "list method" of thinking. It left no room for shades of gray in its matter-of-fact black and white manner. What lay before her was truly abstract. A stranger would give up his body to Spirit for the purposes of physical congress with an adherent. That act could take many levels—but she felt certain her foray would include full intercourse and multiple orgasms. There would be witnesses to the devotional acts. Traditional, but just a tad unnerving. Safety first. Condoms, always. Blood play, never. So much depended upon what agreements were made beforehand between god and horse and horse and devotee and priest or priestess. The rite might be considered a "scene," as in role playing or bondage/discipline venues. But it wasn't role playing. It was a communion of Spirit and human that was as old as the horizon. Seriously, as she and her sister liked to joke, it was dyed-in-the-wool old-time religion.

The self-depreciating thoughts flowed like cream into coffee. *He's a stranger. He's my sister's boyfriend. Most people would consider it an insult to accept money for sex. But it isn't exactly money for sex. They need the closing fees. My patron wished me to offer said funds. In our circles, it isn't unusual for polyamorous relationships to develop and goodness, at Beltane, the cuddle room could bring on a whole new level of rise and shine. I'm not looking for love. I'm not looking to get laid. I date. I've had relationships. No. Who am I fooling? Gods, I can't do this. I'm too shy. I've watched the rituals, but never participated in one. I can't do this. What if he turns me down because he finds me unattractive? I'm Chari's twin, and we may look alike, but we are far from identical. Oh, jeez...he's never met me. Except as an apparition. We know nothing about each other. Except through social media. And through Chari.*

Her phone chirped. She read the text and all breath left her body. *He said maybe. He's under a tremendous amount of stress, and I'm just going to let him take the reins here. He knows we have a time limit. He knows we have additional ways to get the money. It's truly a matter between Loki and him.*

Verity wasn't sure how she should react. *Maybe* was not a *no*. Excited as hell? Reserved? She left the cafeteria and sequestered herself in a vestibule where she felt safe to talk. She pressed the telephone symbol and rang her sister. "I don't want this to come off like an act of prostitution. You know?"

"No problem, Ver. He needs to decide if he's ready to take that step as a priest. He made the verbal plea that he'd sell anything to get the restaurant—and Spirit listens. We briefly discussed that the funds will be a gift to the 501C3. Not to me directly, or to him. No one is tossing cash on the bed after the act."

"When?"

"Johnny and I are hitting a restaurant supply show next weekend and have some appointments with vendors. Thank you for this. It will lift you from academia and into a sacred space from which new insights shall manifest."

Verity's stomach churned. "A bit unusual, this."

"Our lives have been unusual since we were conceived, sis. We'll chat soon. Love you!"

Verity ended the call. "Love you, too."

Chapter Five

Across two state lines into another time zone, Johnny realized he was biting his lip. Deep thoughts. Stressful thoughts. Moving. Drawing down. He almost wished he hadn't burned all his witchcraft initiatory items now. Might have been something in that chest that would offer comfort. *I love Charity. I have wanted this restaurant forever. This is a good thing. It will afford us the funds we need at closing without having to go further into debt. I have never seriously considered being a sacred sex pistol, but damn. I can do this. Oh, dear gods...maybe I can't.* He scrolled through his email. "Notification of electronic deposit from employer." *Good. Payday.* He'd given notice to the resort. He had been head chef at a progressive, organic, Michelin Star, all-inclusive, star-studded guest list, health and well-being clinic for just shy of six years. He'd been content, until he met Charity. She was a woman on a mission, and he'd signed up for the march through the desert. It wasn't ideal—but there was no ideal. She fit the bill. He liked their long-distance relationship. When they were together, it was fireworks all the way. She completed him. The empty parts seemed less empty, and she took care of him, when for so long, he hadn't even been able to take care of himself. And...he cooked with invigorated inspiration when she stood in his kitchen. Magic. He cooked, and they ate until every dish was dirty and their bellies were distended. They were together a few weeks at a time. They fell in love. They made plans. Charity was single-minded. She wanted *Revived Intimacy,* and somehow, his desire to be a restaurateur married her dream and the issue of that love was imminent. They were having a baby. A baby born of mirepoix and goose fat. Phyllo and Sofrito. A baby swaddled in old-time religion and elder gods. *Would you like to offer your orgasm to Aphrodite or Freyja as you enjoy your dessert?*

He took a breath and opened his work email on his phone. Distributors, growers, the cheese man. His employer. *A response to my formal notice, perhaps.* I've given him thirty days, and a list of qualified replacements. *This shouldn't be too bad. He'll whine. He always whines.*

Johnny scrolled up the screen, perusing the email. "Holy shit."

He dashed to his desk, hitting his thigh hard against the edge of the table in his carelessness. He awakened his computer. Type. Password. Wrong. He typed again. Wrong. He took a breath and slowly typed his pass phrase. The computer whirred and hummed and opened by default to his inbox.

He couldn't concentrate on the email. One sentence, both bolded and underlined, said it all. "In breach of non-competition clause." *Did I sign one?* There was an attachment. He clicked it and it downloaded. Highlighted in bright yellow, though scanned a bit off center, were his initials by the non-compete agreement. A tri-state area for one year. Johnny sank into a sectional near his desk. *I am so screwed. Oh shit. Charity is screwed. We are screwed.* He envisioned himself bending over the sofa having the rolled contract shoved up his rear end. "I need a drink."

Johnny poured himself a stiff one. Two fingers of Colkegan Single Malt whiskey, neat. Way earlier in the day than he usually imbibed. He just wanted to take a moment. Chill. Forego panic. He printed the email and attachment and sat back to read it carefully, tumbler in hand. He had forgotten about the non-compete clause. *Maybe I can get it nullified by tossing some money at it. Just about every cent I have is tied up in the move and business.* Not that he was able to contribute as much as Charity to the building and restaurant. She had an inheritance. He had sweat equity in most things. And a bankruptcy still on his credit report. The ex had left him high and dry when she'd absconded with everything some seven years prior. It was moments like this he wished he stayed with the department another few years. He'd been a cop. Walked away from that mess. Cashed out his retirement and took some time off to learn how to sleep again. PTSD sucked. What he saw—what he did. He'd been witness to the worst of the worst. Never a dull moment. He nearly lost hope in humanity and the power of his own soul. It broke up his relationships with his woman, his parents, most of his friends. A man should not become numb to the horrific violence enacted by his brethren. It was when the blood didn't turn his stomach he knew it was time to leave. So leave, he did.

Cooking had been his salvation. Creating something both beautiful and nourishing of body and soul had been a penitent act. Ten years on the force. Ten years a chef. And now, all dreams put on hold for lack of funds to buy his way out of a fucking non-compete.

He looked around his condo. It would go up for sale—probably at a loss. Damn market. He had some antiques.

Already for sale. His personal knife set. Worth thousands. *Can't sell that.* The copper cookware. Another three-grand invested. *My dick. Worth a fortune if I give control of it over to a rambunctious god for an evening. Is any of this worth prostituting myself? Is any of this worth bedding a woman, even in sacred space, that I have never met? Am I crazy to stand upon a moral pedestal when I can alleviate the financial burden by sexual congress?*

He turned back to his laptop and clicked open the email to reply to his employer. *How much do you want me to pay to get out of this?* Send.

Johnny had a headache. A big one. He needed to eat. He pressed the pizza delivery app on his phone. He wasn't cooking tonight. And if he couldn't get out of the non-compete, he might not be cooking in his own place—ever. Pessimistic, perhaps. A text reply gave him a forty-minute delivery time. Not too bad. He nursed his drink and reclined into the chair. He closed his eyes.

A familiar pressure annoyed the back of his skull like a child tapping on glass. Spirit knocking. Wasn't his first time at the chili cookoff. He placed his feet solidly upon the concrete floor and straightened his back. He allowed the tendrils of divine energy to infiltrate his body. He breathed slowly...in...out. This was an act of faith. Of trust. Opening himself to listen to his gods. Or at least the most talkative one. He saw old Flame Hair in the veil. He approached with grace of a dancer. Each step was deliberate, precise and smooth. His tall, lithe body seemingly twirled with flame as it cascaded from his head to the ethereal ground. He spoke first. "Hello, Loki."

Never one to mince words when it came to affairs of the heart, Loki laughed and sidled up to Johnny in the ethers. "Do it! I want it. Do it for the money. Do it to honor me." Loki's long red braid whipped him in the face like a horse tail against a fly.

"I'm not comfortable with it," Johnny replied.

"Get comfortable."

"Should not this type of work be from a place of fullness and not scarcity? The whole selling my body for sex thing unnerves me." Johnny brushed Loki's hair away. The braid slithered like a serpent. It had a mind of its own.

"It is the easiest money you'll ever make. I can make it worth your while."

"How so?"

Loki shifted into a more professional appearance, contract in hand. Business suit. Short hair. Wildness in eyes slightly subdued. "Make love to her. Certainly, you know how to arouse a woman, no? Secure the funds. And I will bless you and yours deeply. Blessings of connection to the food. Connection to the consumers. Connection to the gods. You think you will run a sustainable business, yes?"

Johnny nodded.

"With my assistance, it will sustain not only in ecological ways, but spiritually economic ways."

"Contract with the devil."

Loki chuckled. "I'm no devil. I'm a god. And you know me. We've worked together before. Have I ever not kept my part of the deal?"

"You've been good to me." Johnny paused. "I just don't know if I can perform with a woman I do not love. With whom

I have no true connection. I'm not twenty any longer. Sex for me is as much a mental activity as a physical one."

Loki tapped on Johnny's head. "Saddle up. She is oathed to me. I love her. I would take her in the flesh and experience the pure bliss of a lover's embrace in her arms. When I move you to hold her, kiss her, pleasure her...your body will respond as a man should respond. I sense you fear you will not be able to perform because there is no love between you. I beg to differ. It is I who shall imbue you with the love necessary for arousal, penetration, and consummation. I know you refuse to lose control in any situation, thereby you may remain as present as you wish. You can choose to remember none of it—or all of it. It's up to you. Think of it as a temperature gauge. Johnny can choose his level of mental participation from ice to rapid boil. Just love her for me. Love her for one night."

"A night to remember, huh?"

"Yes."

Johnny chuckled. "Is that not the name of a movie about the sinking of the *Titanic*?"

"It is. But this is no disaster. This is a melding of mortal flesh with divine intent. It is an offering. An act of worship—for me to worship her. For her to honor me. And though you feel moral restrictions with the act, it will be a blessing."

"A blessing in disguise, Loki. You are a true trickster. To allow you a full ride—it is a bit unnerving. I must know that I can implicitly trust you. As you said, I'm kind of a control freak."

"We can contract that. A high level of trust is assured. We Norse deities are nothing, if not honorable in business."

"All right. Let me mull this over."

"Then wake up, sir. Or you'll spill your glass."

A GENTLE RAP ON THE door awakened Johnny. He glanced at his cell phone. Fifty minutes had passed. He'd fallen asleep. And been visited. He rose. *No matter how much Loki may want me to perform a sacred sexual rite, it is up to me. Free will.*

In the dark recesses of his mind, he heard Loki's voice chide, *Fuck free will. You have a great cock for a human. Pleasure my woman. Use your entire body to pleasure her, and I will use my godly influence to enhance your mundane life. It seems a win-win situation to me.*

Johnny smirked. Being god-touched was not always a blessing. He shrugged. At least he knew it wasn't schizophrenia. Though there *is* a fine line between divinity and madness.

He mechanically ate his pizza. He was too tired and too overwrought to "Yelp" about flavor, consistency, and overall value. Nourishment was all he needed. Something to fill his belly and keep him from freaking out. He surfed over to Facebook. *Verity accepted my friend request. Wow. All right. This is so strange. How do you talk to a woman about sacred intercourse? And should this sacred act be borne of the desperation our financial shortfall has thrust upon us? It doesn't feel like I'm making this decision from a good place. Do I get over it, take one for the team, and ignore the churning of my stomach?* He opened a message window. And promptly closed it.

The image of an ostrich burying its head in the sand flashed before his eyes. *Good idea. Ignore the monster and maybe it will ignore you. If I don't contact her or ever speak of this matter, it's not real. Said the fool.*

Chapter Six

Charity made lists. She and Verity differed in process, but one of their shared twin traits was "listing." She'd been moving away from sticky notes—which then ended up as photos in her phone because she habitually took snaps of them—rather than actually using a "to do" app. She noted that her plans all stopped in the same place. *Get the money needed for closing.* This was a blockage she needed to blow the hell up before she could walk away like a boss. Once signed, everything else would be so much cake. Johnny would cook. She'd run the front. Hire minimal staff and offer simple meals—family style—to begin. Her *women in business start-up grant* would pay for stock and advertising. And she knew she could make that money last. Plus, she already had verbal contracts with various business owners to supply tiffin-style lunches to their workers. Bento boxes, maybe. It would vary, day to day. Each container sent out was a "return for deposit" situation. An employee would deliver the lunches and pick up the empties on a rotating basis. If it could work in Mumbai and Tokyo, it could work in the Pacific Northwest. One protein, one starch, one veggie, and a small dessert. And best of all, *Reviving Intimacy* would receive a percentage for each meal sold.

"Breakthrough." Intention set, she pricked her finger and placed a drop of blood at the base of a candle wick. She then sprinkled the candle with sugar and lit it. A simple spell of sympathetic magic to appease the gods of commerce and hospitality. *Perhaps I should throw in a "hail Loki," since it is his essence that will move Johnny's body and line my wallet. It does sound a bit dubious, this sacred sex business. But I know it is not. My priests and priestesses will draw down and offer healing to patrons—by word, thought, and deed. By touch. And it doesn't have to be a sexual touch. Intimacy is so much more than sharing body parts. The first time a priestess of Aphrodite touched my shoulders I knew this was my calling. Divine connection and interaction. One size does not fit all. But am I to be all-inclusive, offering Charismatic snake-handling to Santeria and everything in between? I shouldn't get ahead of myself. I'll let the gods speak. Hard to make a schedule when you don't know which god wants to offer what on which day.* She added a memo under her "contracts" tab. *Get binding contracts with deities for services.*

Her cell phone vibrated. She detested ring tones and chirping sounds. *It's Johnny.* "Hey, handsome."

"Hi, Chari."

"Oh, Johnny—what's going on? I can tell by the tone in your voice something is up."

"Two words spoken and you can read me like a book. You know me so well, babe."

"Spill it." She looked at her "breakthrough" spell. *That was fast.* "Whatever it is, we can handle it."

"I signed a non-compete," he replied.

"This morning?"

That made him laugh. "No. I gave notice, and then the Big Boss sent me a copy of my contract. I don't recall there being a non-compete clause, but there is. One year, tri-state area. He knows how good I am. He was afraid, even back then, that I was going to branch out on my own."

"And this means what to us? Speak plainly." Chari didn't like the edge in her voice. *Johnny has PTSD. He isn't keen on confrontation.* She rephrased quickly. "How will this affect our plans, babe?"

"I can probably buy my way out of the contract. His favorite green isn't the organic kind, if you know what I mean."

"We're already short—how much more will this set us back?" Chari again corrected the edge on her voice.

"Yeah...about that. I know I could do it, but I'm not sure the ritual should be born of scarcity. I'm uncomfortable with..."

Chari bit her lip. "No problem." *No problem at all. Fuck.*

"Can I finish?" he asked.

Attitude in check. Tone of voice calm. "Yes, please."

"I want to do it. I just don't know if I can do it. Loki is kind of a hard ride. I'm with you, Chari. I don't want to be with another woman. I mean...I know it's not like having a fling or affair. The entire intention is not for me to receive personal gratification, even though I know I will. It's about what is best for you and me, and our dream."

"It's your choice. I'm sure we will come up with all the funds we need to close and get you out of indentured servitude. Did you reach out to Loki? Do a little divination or meditate?"

"I yelled at him. It worked. He is all for it. Naturally."

Chari realized her fist was clenched. "Well, I do love the Norse gods—they can be so approachable from time to time. But, my love, what will be, will be."

"Don't get all fatalistic on me, Chari."

She cleared her throat, not wanting to make a reply.

Johnny continued. "I can't talk to your sister about this. I don't know her well enough. Certainly not well enough to know her in a Biblical sense. Or whatever Loki calls relations with his mortal wives." He paused. "Charity...breathe. You're not breathing."

"I'm fine. It's fine. I believe in this project and I know the gods are behind me. We'll figure something out."

"I could stay here a while longer. I make a good wage. If I don't travel back and forth to see you as often and make a few other cuts, I could save thousands in a year." Johnny knew this would not fly with Chari.

"I can't get an extension. We can't get an extension. Maybe I should put my place up for sale and live in the building."

"There's a thought. But I don't want you to sell your house, babe. We are going to need somewhere away from the business to regroup. Will your sister loan you the money anyway?"

Charity coughed. "I don't want to owe her money. It was actually cleaner when it was a gift for a gift—at least in my eyes—and probably in hers."

"I'm sorry. Don't say anything just yet, all right? Let me see how things pan out here."

"I want you with me, Johnny. I want us together. I love you. Let's not consider your postponing the move."

He rarely said the words. He felt them. He believed in them. But saying them...hard as hell. "Love you, too." Like fucking pulling teeth.

Chari heard it in his voice. It surprised her that he made a *réponse de l'amour. Fuck, he'd open a vein and bleed out before doing anything that fell under the "romance" category.*

Chapter Seven

Verity looked at Johnny's social media profile. Again. *This opportunity means more to me than I am willing to admit to my sister—or even myself. Scientifically, sociologically, sexually—this is huge. He is attractive, I'll give him that. Though Loki would have to horse Donald Trump to give me pause. Whoa! Not going there. I can't look at Johnny's profile picture without seeing Loki's wicked grin superimposed.* She tapped on the message button. A chat screen opened. *Can we talk about this? Verity.* Send. "Holy shit. Have I now opened a can of worms or the gates to the underworld?"

I am a woman of both faith and science. I have relied on theoretical evidence and observational methods thus far, but there's no reason I cannot engage in empirical research. Hands on, so to speak. She recalled her mother's words, *Look with your eyes, not with your hands.* She pursed her lips—hard. *Fuck that. It's time I wrote the book on sacred sexuality, and that means I need to get my hands dirty.* She patted herself on the back. *I heretofore accept I must move beyond my smaller self, tell fear to bugger off, and g'head and run with some of my deluded impulses. Should the opportunity arise. Literally. I will come out on top. Again, literally.* Verity took a breath and began making notations on the white board for her next class.

A confidence born of facing fear and change head-on kept a spring in her step through class. Bless the underclassman who brought cookies. She had two. She wanted four. She felt grateful she had thirty minutes to herself at the end of her day. She called it a "rogue prep," because it generally equated to her creating lesson plans with the pace of a herd of wildebeests in panic-mode. Or perhaps with the vigor of a hungry male hippo in rut. If anyone interrupted her during this time, she was certain she'd bite of their feet. And she was hungry. Her entire being ached to be filled. The prospect of holding her patron—her Beloved—in-body...emptied her of all but need. The night she had oathed to Loki, he had come to her in a semi-viscous state. Not solid. Not as an apparition. He moved across her slowly, as if he were made of honey, and caressed every part of her. When they consummated their agreement, his cock had felt solid enough. One thrust inside her and she experienced an orgasm that cascaded up and over and out the crown of her head. He left her, in a stupor, in bed. Wet with sweat.

To experience that depth of passion in the flesh...to feel a man's body pressed against hers and know that the spirit moving it was truly joined with her—on every level—*miraculous*. She shuddered. She wanted to make a vague social media post. *#want*. Simply...*#want*. Would that be too bold? Would Johnny see it and know it was his horsed body she craved? Would Chari see it and tease her later? Would anyone even care? Social media was a snake pit at best.

Chapter Eight

Johnny read the message from Verity and, as with most things he did not have capacity to deal with, did not reply. "I do not have the spoons to deal with the sale of my cock right now."

He began to obsessively check his email. A high level of impatience preceded each refresh. He paced. He drummed his fingers. He poured. He drank. He taunted his pizza. *Perhaps I should lay off the sauce for now. Back-talking to a slice of pizza is not helping.*

The stressors of his life seemed to be plaguing him in numerous adverse ways. The pit of his stomach ached. He had a headache. His shoulders hurt. His breastbone hurt. The big toe of his left foot throbbed as if he'd stubbed it. He finished another shot and refreshed his email again.

Aaaannnddddd...bingo. Boss man has replied. The pain in his gut and head increased exponentially. His hand trembled as he clicked open the email. His ticket offshore was going to cost... *10k.*

Johnny turned and withheld the urge to vomit. He made it to the kitchen trash can before expelling the booze and pizza. *Ten thousand dollars. Fuck me. Is it negotiable? Can I make payments? Should I hire a lawyer? I do not want to hire a lawyer. I want to walk away from this and move to Washington with*

Chari. Can I just skip out and let him catch up with me later? No. That could jeopardize the business. I'm a legal part-owner. Unless I take my name off everything. I can't do that. Can I do that? Maybe I do need an attorney. Fuck.

He rinsed his mouth and returned to the open email. "Oh, great. I missed the provisos." He increased the font using the little slide tool on the lower right. The headache had become nearly blinding. "Payment in full must be received in certified funds no later than twenty-four hours from the final date of employment. This offer of settlement is final and non-negotiable. Attached please find a business loss statement that covers Hacienda Valhalla's projected expenses in replacing you and training and acclimating staff to a new head chef. And my projection is generous. There are some regular clients who will be hesitant to make long-term reservations knowing that their favorite chef has departed."

Johnny hung his head and swallowed the lump in his throat. Ten thousand dollars. Ten thousand dollars, plus the four we need at closing. A cartoon image of Loki popped into his head. Loki, holding the problem in one hand, and the solution in the other. All one had to do was get past everything that lay in between the right and left. He held out his hands before him, palm up. Short of using those open hands for begging, how was he to obtain this exorbitant amount of money? What lay between his own hands? The problem and the solution. He brought his hands together before his crotch in the shape of an upright V. *Hold a Lokean tent revival and let him screw me out of this mess.*

Maybe it was the booze. Maybe the stress. But the idea sounded better and better with each passing moment. *How many of Loki's women are there who would pay to be with him in-body? How many can I satisfy physically while being possessed by the spirit of a very potent Norse god? And what am I doing thinking that only women would want to be with him? I haven't taken a foray into bi-sexuality yet, but I'm not opposed. How does one advertise this without drawing the wrong kind of attention? Would we take out an ad on Craigslist? On the dark net? Word of mouth, only. Would I have to be the only person to draw down? How many can he inhabit at the same time? Would Loki jump from vessel to vessel to use the time most effectively? And what about the test? Would each vessel need to consume chili pepper liqueur, or something like that to establish true possession? We'd need three or four legitimate channels and have a handler or two for each of them, protein and water, and we really can't do it outside.* Johnny paused his rapid-fire, alcohol-fueled thoughts. "Can you rise to the occasion, little buddy?" He patted his crotch. "Can the stallion service the herd?" He felt a twinge of arousal at the passing thought of servicing a half-dozen adoring ladies. Large breasts, small breasts, thick booties, long legs, black hair, fucking bald. *I won't care. It will be all about what Loki wants.*

Johnny slid his right hand into his drawstring pants and wrapped his fingers around his burgeoning erection. *You want this, Loki? You want to possess my cock and go around the world with a few of your most adoring fans?* He gave his dick a few pulls. Needed lube. This was a special occasion. Only the best. He strolled into the kitchen, his cock bumping out the front of his pants, and reached for the Lambda Ultra Premium Extra Virgin. He pulled his pants down to his thighs and poured a capful into his hand. It was a chef thing—knowing his right hand was slathered with $200.00 per bottle olive oil was better than porn. The floral scent of the oil intoxicated him even more than the alcohol had. And he couldn't hold a titillating image in his mind as he stroked his hand. He certainly had the physical arousal to orgasm. Mentally...not so much. He picked a fantasy. He didn't want to waste the liquid gold and not get something out of it other than slick. Pressure was on. If he didn't rub this one out now, his frustration level would stay at defcon 3.

He had never been much for watching porn. His imagination was generally enough to get the juices flowing. He had a couple of favorite fantasies. And when he and Chari had first hooked up—it had all been so new and wonderful that thoughts of her, alone, could get him off. Thoughts of her wrapped in his arms were both arousing and comforting. She was "the one." The one he loved. Worth this move. Worth it all.

That did the trick. It wasn't ultimately satisfying, but it took the edge off. He released into a paper towel, hiked up his pants, then washed his hands. He recorked the olive oil. He again enthroned it upon the kitchen counter. All hail the king of oils.

That was not altogether refreshing, the additional voice in his head commented.

"Not now, Loki," he replied.

It could be that you need to reconnect with your spiritual side before you will achieve true satisfaction.

Johnny inwardly cursed being god-touched. "Are you threatening me?"

I never make threats.

"I don't appreciate being coerced," Johnny replied.

Nor do I coerce. I make promises. And I keep them.

Johnny sat at his computer and surfed over to his investments website. "I am not trickster bait. I am not at the end of a line, bobbing up and down in the fishing hole of the gods. I don't want to contact her. Not right now."

Good thing I'm patient, Loki replied.

Johnny mulled over the situation. His predicament. The ramifications if he did not perform in ceremony and the potential benefits if he did. His gut told him that he didn't want to become involved in a Loki-fueled act of sacred sexuality. *And yet, I am in love with a woman who seeks to revive intimacy by way of mortal connection to Spirit. Fuck it. There must be another way. I can cash out my whole life policy. Net value is about seven thousand. I wonder if I can counter with that, regardless of what the email said. I am already going to lose money on this condo and in wages and now, scramble my nest egg. I might as well just bend over and allow the universe to sodomize me with the pointy stick of poverty now and get it over with.* He opened the email from Hacienda Valhalla. The gods help them who help themselves. He typed, *Thank you for your reply. I respectfully counter with 5K.*

He hit send, hoping to keep a little money under his wing. Maybe toss it into the closing costs.

He waited for the sky to fall. But not before pinging Verity. "This just adds another level of crazy to my life. I need some time."

Chapter Nine

Verity hesitated upon seeing the pop-up message from Johnny appear on her social media screen. If she didn't open it—didn't read it—there was still a chance she would soon participate in a ritual that would not only be personally satisfying but academically enlightening. Of course, ignoring the message would just prolong the agony. *Prolonged agony. So...Lokean of me. Am I enjoying this? The uncertainty of it all? No. Not really. I like things lined up. Ducks in a row. No stone left unturned. I don't like surprises or adventures I have not vetted.* After several minutes, she opened the message. Reading it did not make her feel any better. The horse was being led to water but was disinclined to drink.

She resisted pinging Chari in complaint. It was her expectations that were shattered—or shattering. Johnny hadn't agreed to the ritual, per se, and he hadn't actually refused yet, either. *The Trickster has my number and is playing to the beat. With my head as the bass drum. So, how do we legitimize this? Do I just give Chari the money and cultivate patience for my reward? Or give Chari the money and forgo any thoughts of sacred sex on this earthly plain?*

"Why give up now?"

Startled, Verity turned to find a very physical male guest to her classroom. Though the door was locked. For a second time, she beheld the playful blue eyes and salt and pepper hair—a reasonable facsimile of Johnny Lightman. *All right…not my first time at the rodeo.* "Hello, Loki."

"Ah, recognition."

"Are you really corporeal, or am I like under a spell or something?"

Loki stretched, and smiled.

Verity posed the question again. "Is this live or is it Memorex?"

"No, I'm not in physical form. You are spirited away to my realm. But have no fear. You are perfectly safe. I cannot stop time, nor can I change the past or revive the dead—but hide between raindrops—or lift your essence to an astral plain of existence…piece of cake. Now, my sweet, I can and will convince old Johnny boy to bed you, and it will be the experience of a lifetime, indeed. He has a fine body, and I have the power of the pure love I feel for you. We shall make a formidable pairing. However, this gift for a gift—this *gebo*—it is between you and I as well as Johnny and me and, well…I suppose I will need to draw your sister into this, too. What contract shall we make, my dear?"

"What do you want? Specifically."

"Offspring," Loki replied flatly.

Verity choked. "Children? Human children? A baby?"

"Specifically, a Nephilim. Godly human hybrid."

"I don't want children right now—especially one I'd end up raising alone."

Loki shook his head. "No, darling. The seed need only be planted in the sweet soil of your body. It will not grow within you. Such issue will ascend to the arms of the mother-gods and will not be a part of the mortal world, but the astral one. Very seldom, indeed, has a mortal woman ever been aware of the conception—in any lore or tradition. Your knowing ahead of time that I would use his body, and your body, to produce a Nephilim is unique."

"I don't know how I feel about that. You want to sire a baby using Johnny's body and your will and let the life take root within me, but then said baby will not be a part of my life. Am I an Easy Bake Oven? A petri dish?"

"You are my mortal wife. I have many, of course, but my attention is fixed here, with you. You are doing interesting things. Things that will serve to ensure my bloodline in the heavens and beyond."

Verity sat atop a two-person table. "You have children. In the lore."

"I have three daughters, Hel, Einmyria and Eisa, and five sons, Fenrir, Jormundgard, Vali, Narvi, Sleipnir. All deity-bred and born. They have no roots in humanity. I also am parent to a myriad of beings—salmon, trolls, flies. I have many children."

Verity ran through the names of Loki's children in mythology. "The daughters of Glow—Ashes and Embers. Then the children of Angrboda—Hel, Fenrir, and Jormungaard. And with Sigyn, Narvi, and Vali. And you are mother to Sleipnir. How many Nephilim have you sired?"

"Two. Twins, now deceased. Long deceased. It was a thousand years ago. Over a thousand years ago. She was a Varangian. Constantinople. I rode—possessed—a magnificent soldier—a Nubian mercenary. He was an animist and worshipped the spirit of the Pink Ivorywood tree. A very powerful spirit. He had no concept of the Aesir gods. I spoke to him in the old tongue of his people, and he willingly accepted me. He was an amazing man. And he sired amazing children, strong and fierce like their mother. They were born warriors. They met with honorable deaths but did not leave children behind. Alas, even godling children can die in battle." Loki began a slow turn about the room. "I wish my bloodline to flourish on Midgard. On earth. My Nephilim children will eventually mix and breed with mortals and from those pairings, my lineage shall continue in the world of humankind. My divine children do not share such a blessed destiny. They shall never walk a mortal plane. I have foreseen it."

"I have concerns about you using the Abrahamic term *Nephilim*. The word is used for the issue of an angel and humans. And you, sir, are no angel."

"It's an adequate word to describe the issue of god and mortal. We have no distinct word in Old Norse. Incorporating words of Judeo/Christian origin is not problematic for us, as we are all a part of the universal spirit."

Verity weighed her options carefully. It was prudent, nay—necessary—to clearly and concretely set out both boundaries and bargains with Loki. "Free will."

Loki scoffed. "What of it?"

"Johnny has it. He might agree to hold me but change his mind. You can't very well specify "no take-backs" when working a *gebo*."

Loki stroked his well-trimmed graying goatee. "I see your point. I will jump off that cliff if the situation arises. But I doubt the involved parties will have a change of heart once we've all come to terms. And then, my sweet, we shall finally rest in each other's arms, completely spent, and sticky with the sweat of love."

"You wax poetic today, Loki. Being with you in-body has long been a wish of mine, but there are so many levels of craziness to the entire act that I feel like I'm journeying through the rings of hell with Dante and Virgil."

"*Dante's Inferno*. I know it well. I have a quote you may relate to...*do not be afraid; our fate cannot be taken from us; it is a gift.*" Still toying with his goatee, Loki continued. "I don't think the act of love—this gift—can be adequately described in human speech. As I've said before, I must learn how to communicate words of love in bird song. It seems the only fitting language to describe the act and emotion."

Verity laughed. "Kuckoo!"

"Will you be the soil in which my divinely inspired child takes root, my sweet?"

"If you can help keep the insanity to a moderate level, I will allow your Nephilim access. But you must promise me that this child will be cared for and loved and not made the instigator in some evil plan."

Loki leaped forward like Baryshnikov and kissed Verity quickly. "Lovely!"

"I used to read romance novels doing my laundry in college. I'd grab them off the free pile at the library. Lots of babies born to save humanity in those books with the awesome clinch covers. I never thought I'd be the heroine with the magic vagina who begets a child who saves the future."

Loki laughed. "Touché!" And with that, as was his usual method of departure, he was gone.

Upon snapping out of Loki's astral venue, Verity looked at the message from Johnny again. *I don't need to do anything. Loki has this. I've never been big on letting go and letting god—but in this case, it's worth a try.*

Chapter Ten

Loki often felt as if he had bitten off more than he could chew. Times like that he needed to clear his head. By booze. By sex. By conversation with a trusted friend. He sat back and slid his hand partway down his pants. *Who am I kidding? I have no friends. I have minions. And lovers. And worshipers and perhaps a few equals, but friends? Probably not.* He rested his hand on the waistband of his yoga pants and glanced longingly at the French Press across the room. He was everywhere, but nowhere. His own little kingdom between worlds to be found only in the bark of a dog, chatter of a squirrel, and purr of a kitten. No hired help. No indentured servants. If he wanted a cup of the dark stuff, he'd have to make it, himself. Laziness enveloped him; he didn't want to move. But the plot needed a thickening agent, and that agent was coffee. Strong, black coffee. At least two cups. No sugar. No whitener. Just hot water and ground beans married into a delicious, furious concoction of drinkable bliss. The beverage of the gods. Coffee. And deep thought. *I have a man to steer, a priestess to keep focused, and a Nephilim to create and true love to send her way.* He mulled over the situation. *I need swift and clear communications. I wonder if I should seek out Hermes. He's always good in a pinch.* He arose and put flame to the kettle.

It was so much easier in days of old to convince a man or woman or otherkin to draw my spirit in for whatever purpose I needed a corporeal body. What, with all this "consent" and "agency" now, a god can't get his cock in the door. Ah, well. Times change, and as Darwin said, "It is not the strongest of species who survives, but the one most adaptable to change." And I am the god of change. Johnny Lightman, I enjoy my communion with you. You are a sarcastic, talented, passionate asshole of a man, and you are what is needed to make my wife and your lover happy. Loki took a breath and sent his spirit out. Little trickster tendrils of persuasion. *An hour of your time, Johnny. That's all I need. Admittedly, I will use your body in ways you are familiar, yet unaccustomed. An hour of your time as sacred consort and you and your woman shall have all the funds you need to revive intimacy. It's a win-win. Give me use of your cock and tongue and fingertips. Give me use of your arms to wrap her in and your thighs to push into her. Give me all of you for one hour. And I shall provide ample opportunity to you and yours.* He paused, then called out to his Greek god counterpart, "Hermes! Fellow trickster and god of communication...open a channel and let this work be done." *Rather like a god praying to a god. Interesting, that. But not the first, nor will it be the last time, such boons have been asked and granted. Even gods get by with a little help from their friends. Oh, maybe I do have a few friends, after all.*

Loki had an "in" with Johnny Lightman. Johnny was one of his people. They'd danced the dance of horse and rider before. Didn't mean Johnny wouldn't ignore the call to action. Free will and all that. Loki closed his eyes and whispered into the darkness beyond the veil, "Johnny. Hear me." He waited for the tremble of his voice across the cosmos to subside. Its echo made him shiver. The soul of the man he wished to reach didn't respond immediately. Like a wick being kissed by a lighter, the reception sputtered before sparking to life. Loki continued, knowing he had hit his target. "Say yes. Say yes and follow through. Do not allow your balls to shrink up into your groin because you perceive this as a stressful situation. You know I will do nothing to harm you or others. Do me a solid, Johnny."

If the heavens were made of sheet music, Loki's call would become notes on both the base and treble clefts, melodic and bold. The sonorous tones sailed on the winds behind the veil, passing through and into realms of humankind. As old as time and always refreshing itself, the pure and far-reaching voices of the gods had never abandoned humankind. Those who listened, heard the call.

Johnny felt the subtle tapping on the back of his head. *Always when I'm in the shower. How does he know?* He pictured himself in a dark theater. It was a trick he'd learned to block everything else out to hear the gods. The screen snapped to life and there he saw Loki, sitting idly. And he heard the message. *He wants this. Nothing new there.* He addressed Loki, aloud. "I'm kind of monogamous, Loki."

Loki turned to face Johnny. "This is not about monogamy or having an affair or other such mortal construct. This is an act of sacred sexuality between two of my people for the benefit of god and human. Nothing need be taken too seriously when the deed is done. You'll be too busy setting up shop and Verity will be head down recording the experience."

"Residual Catholic upbringing."

"Fuck that," Loki replied. "Say yes and give us all what we want. What we really want."

"The choice is mine."

"Yes. Always." Loki waved his hand and created a little ball of flame in his palm. "Johnny...please make your choice."

All right, Loki. I'm making my choice. And it is my choice. Johnny stepped out of the shower, dried off, and still naked, picked up his cell phone. He went to his social media app and to Verity's profile. He brought up a private message and hit the camera. The application whirred into action and rang Verity's phone.

Verity's phone chimed. Instant panic. It was Johnny. She looked at the ignore and accept buttons for a split second, then hit green for go. "I'm in. I always figured I'd get pimped out somehow—but I thought it would be with cooking."

Verity held her breath and exhaled sharply. She replied to the message. "Okay." She ended the call.

Instinctively, she began a silent count down. If Johnny had pinged her, then most certainly he had contacted Charity. One. Two. Three. Four. Five.

Her phone chimed a second time almost immediately. *Well, that took less than ten seconds. What Loki wants, Loki gets.*

Verity had to hold the phone away from her ear. "He's in!" Charity calmed her voice. She realized she sounded like an eighth-grade girl. Verity took another breath and replied to her sister. "When?"

"Devil's in the details. We can chat soon. Need ducks in a row. Ritual space made ready."

Verity didn't have words. "Okay." And she ended the call. Twenty minutes later, Verity's innards started behaving like a freeway cloverleaf. Knots. Congestion. Back firing. Not pretty, considering she was about to get naked with a stranger. She chastised herself. Really, no need stress out. This was not a hook-up or date. She spoke aloud, addressing no one in particular. Addressing any god or spirit listening. "I've never read that an act of sacred sexuality required shorn legs and underarms. I assume anything I do, I do for myself, because Loki certainly doesn't have qualms about body hair, dimpled flesh, or perceived imperfections. It would be a courtesy to the vessel if I am clean and well-groomed, of course. And vise-versa. Goodness knows I wouldn't want him snapping out of possession because I have onion breath." *Am I the offering or the priestess? Am I a supplicant, petitioner, respondent, or lamb on a spit? Am I a john and he a sacred whore and my sister, the pimp? Can I relax enough to do this? Can he give up control long enough to let the spirit move him? And I mean really move him. Damn...if I'm doing this I want foreplay. I am not just going to lay back and let him penetrate me, bounce a few times and come. But do I want to make it last all night? What if I come and then can't get aroused again and he's got a furious tumescence? Lube. There must be lube. And rest breaks? Fuck. I need to step back and look at this from a non-emotional point of view. How do I stop Loki if he wants to go from ass to mouth to vag and back again? In astral sex, it doesn't matter. No bacterial hitchhikers. Loki gets crazy sometimes. I wonder if that will come through with Johnny. We'll need a condom squad commander ready to deploy the latex as we progress around the world. Do we need to show our health card? Will there be fluid exchange? I mean...kissing...and what if he performs cunnilingus or I, fellatio? Now I'm just worrying. I should be more centered about this and allow it to happen organically. Or just give my sister the money she needs and walk away and never think about this again. Fucking hell. I need this. I need the experience. I want it.*

She heard a low rumble vibrate through her house. The lights flickered. *Yep, he wants it, too. I need to talk to him. Loki!* She called out with her mind. The pressure of the air in the room didn't change. Loki hadn't heeded the call. "I know of a way to get his attention."

Verity stripped as she wandered into her bedroom. I need to calm down and get the flutters in my belly quieted. She slipped into the flannel sheets of her bed and then reached into the little fabric-covered box on her nightstand. She withdrew her vibrator and a can of olive oil cooking spray. One shot onto the pink silicone and she flipped the switch. She got comfy and allowed herself to sink into the act of self-pleasure. The lube made her slick; ready. She slipped the toy inside and pressed the shaft against her clit. It didn't take long for her to reach climax. Holding the vibrator hard to keep from dislodging it, she exploded in orgasm. And called his name. "Loki!"

That did it.

He loves it when sexual energy is sent his way. She felt him stirring in the ethers.

I heard your call and thank you for the energy, beloved. How can I help you? Loki appeared in her mind as a lithe dancer with hair of flames.

"You know exactly how you can help me," she replied. "Is this some lesson in patience? A gift of the trickster?"

No. It is as it seems. You have honored me so greatly for many years and have never let me come to you in-body. He is a lovely meat-suit, and our congress shall be memorable.

Verity fell into Loki's arms. They fit perfectly. Their bodies melded. "I'm afraid," she whispered.

Of course you are. Lay your fears to rest. I will not let anything harmful come to you.

"Except a Nephilim."

Chapter Eleven

It took thirteen days to come to an agreement as to a date for the ceremony. Lucky thirteen. The morning before they'd set the date, she'd seen it play out in a dream. *There is not enough alcohol in the world to get me through this.*

List-addicted twins, there would be nothing untoward brought to a head. Some rituals were free flowing, some rife with constraint. This would be the latter. One does not give Loki a lot of leeway. Something might burn down. With him, boundaries were necessary.

Verity looked at the list from her sister. "Loki hates rituals."

"Johnny, too. But in this case, I think the formality is needed. Let's go over this." The video chat fluttered. Charity laughed. "Control your divine husband, sis. Tell him to quit screwing with our connection. We need to get through this."

"Control Loki? All right. I'll try." Verity laughed. She then read the bulleted points on their shared list.

You, Johnny, and I are to meet at the home of Sam Riddermark next Saturday at noon.

I'm bringing the coffee and coffeemaker, because Sam does not drink coffee.

You will bring the half-n-half and honey for Johnny's coffee.

Johnny and I will meet and have informal discussion over snacks. We will then retire to a private area to go over our lists of likes and dislikes and sexual preferences. We may shake hands, but not hug. We may not kiss until a circle is cast."

Charity chimed in. "That first kiss in a sacred sexual union can pack a wallop. I need to know that you two are still conscious before I shut the door behind me."

"Right." Verity continued. "I shall invite Loki into the conversation, but Johnny will not aspect him at that time. One of us, or both of us, will hear and speak for Loki—if he chooses to put his two cents in."

"And after the ritual, you will make your generous donation to Revived Intimacy, LLC. Then probably toddle off to make clinical notes about the experience. I know you. You won't hangout if there's a paper to write."

"Right you are. I assume the aftercare will proceed without a hitch and that I will be able to head home within an hour or so." Verity scribbled a few notes about what she thought she might need for aftercare. Besides a shower, coffee, and possibly a rock or tree root to hold to siphon off any extra godly energy she carried out from the heart of the ritual space. "You are going to act as handler for both Johnny and me? Hard to do when you are priestessing."

"Johnny's brother is coming in to help. He used to work the psychic fair circuit and knows how to ground vessels."

"Okay. See you soon. Love you, Chari."

"Love you, too."

And that was it. The production was scheduled. The cast on-board and blessings from the gods secured. Verity felt fairly confident that Loki would not bow out due to his desire to have a half-mortal child. Nor would Loki allow Johnny to get cold feet for the exact same reason. The Nephilim. A child *that I shall never meet. One I shall never hold.* Verity whispered to Loki, knowing he was never far away, "I want to be fulfilled in love and marriage on this mortal plain, Loki. I'd like children someday. Ones that I can raise."

LOKI WAS CLOSE. HE heard. He knew her heart. *There is no "Tinder of the gods," per se. No personals ads for god-touched academics. She works too much and is far too introverted to meet a mate using conventional means. She needs someone who understands her path but is independent enough to give her space when she needs it, companionship when she needs it, and the stiff one as often as she wants it. I do so love playing matchmaker.* He had great vision. It wasn't ocular, per se. It was, however, far reaching. He looked across the worlds for a glimmer of mortal connection—Verity's soul mate. He existed. Loki felt certain of that fact. His gaze fell in concentric circles spiraling out from Verity's heart. He startled as he perceived that special glow surrounding a man not too far from her home. He laughed. "Well, this is unexpected and so rich. Delicious. Oh, Hermes, when I ask you to open communications, you certainly do come through."

Chapter Twelve

Verity had been living with butterflies and night sweats. She checked her list four times before finally starting her car. A line from a *Mad Max* movie came to mind. *Everything marked. Everything 'memered.* Yeah. I got this. I am about to experience, firsthand, that which I have written and taught about for a long time. Firsthand. I am going to make love with my Patron. In body. She had not wanted to feel attraction to Johnny. This was not about how handsome he was. How bloody lucky her sister was. No. This was about helping them both achieve a goal. It was for her and her career. It was to honor Loki. She giggled. So many pagans were afraid to even hail Loki for fear of inviting the world breaker persona into their midst. Poppycock. *You get the Loki you call. If you expect the sword's edge, you get cut. If you expect the worst, he will certainly provide just that. If you expect the parent, the lover, the magician or trickster, he complies. Just be ready to accept the consequences of any of his aspects that you call. His cunning runs deep.* She took a breath, poised to turn over the ignition. "Hail Loki. Thank you for this opportunity. Thank you for respecting our free will and for laying the foundation for us to achieve our goals. It is our work that brings reward. It is your fire that lights our path."

She listened to the wind outside her car. It spoke to her as richly as any sign and wonder of the gods. *Hail Verity, beloved mortal wife. Teacher, priestess, adventurer. Sometimes you choose your gods, and sometimes we choose you. I choose you. I am honored to be in your life.*

"Thank you, Loki. I need to turn off the god phone now. Can't very well drive if I'm concentrating on chatter from the ethers."

See you soon, beloved.

She started her car and pulled away from her safety zone. Everything she knew was about to change. Become clearer. Heightened. Concrete. Nothing theoretical in actually sleeping with a spirit-possessed man. Only fear and societal norms stood in the way of this being the most amazing experience of her life. Fear can be quelled. And the constructs of society toppled. Verity briefly clenched her right hand into a fist and envisioned a punch to the head of a Puritan forefather.

Traffic sucked. She had to go pee but didn't want to deviate from her mission to drive four hours south to the Riddermark house. Finally, the call of nature was too strong, and she pulled off the interstate, found a restroom, and got a cuppa. The earthquake in her belly had hardly subsided. In fact, the closer she got to her destination, the more pronounced it became. She bought a pack of antacids and got back on the freeway. Her GPS told her to head in the opposite direction. Of course it did. Of course. She ignored the app's British male voice instructing her to take a U-turn and run in the opposite direction and proceeded south. "Nope. I'm doing this Mr. GPS. I'm not listening to you. I am going to go through with it."

Arguing with a phone app was not her finest hour.

JOHNNY FLEW IN. CHARITY picked him up at the airport and then drove him to her place. They made love. The restaurant show hadn't panned out. Both looked forward to time together in a hotel room—but their bodies were desperate for release. They didn't make it to bed. Johnny took her up against the closed front door. A deep kiss was all that was needed to arouse them to readiness. Chari dropped to her knees and unfastened his belt buckle to withdraw his hard cock. She slid her lips around it and took it as far as she could down her throat. "Chari," he whispered, lifting her. They kissed again, and he slid one clever hand between her legs to hike up her skirt and pull her panties off. He lowered his mouth to her cleavage and manipulated her clitoris.

"Now, Johnny. I need you inside me now." Chari reached for his cock. He obliged her.

She was not a small woman, but 160lbs was nothing for him. He had strong arms and solid legs. He lifted her and pressed against her to hold her in place. She opened herself to him, and he slid inside her.

Chari positioned her body to make sure that each thrust hit her clitoris. She came first, burying her head into his shoulder to stifle her cries. He thrust a few times into her wetness and climaxed deep inside her. "I love you," he sighed. "I love you."

Chari giggled. "Well, that's new."

They separated and walked toward the bathroom. "I know. I don't say it often enough. But I do, and I need you to know it."

"I know it, babe. I know it."

After showering and a quick call out for Chinese, Charity wanted to get down to brass tacks. She called up the list—her sacred list. Johnny scrolled through it, pursing his lips.

"Say something, babe."

"This is quite thorough. My brother is an experienced handler, though he doesn't actively participate in ritual these day. You how, Chai, this list will certainly be, if nothing else, amusing. You know you can't really put the gods into a bulleted list. Especially not the Norse gods. Loki, in particular. I think the only thing you can really control are the actions you take. Calling the directions, securing wards. Setting the magical intention. As for the gods and vessels...I cannot guarantee that I will follow a script. Loki is anything but academic."

"This needs to be a safe and sane venture. There needs to be some sort of format so Verity can grasp it linearly. Abstracts are difficult for her."

"Sweetie—you cannot expect A-Z. Loki is likely to start at J and bounce around the alphabet however he wishes. And I've agreed to go along for the ride."

"Well. We'll see." She paused. "When does your brother arrive?"

"He is flying in the day of. And then he'll leave right after. He is a busy man."

"He has his own plane. He can come and go when and where he wants."

"Can we agree to allow Loki some leeway with the ritual so he doesn't start seriously coloring outside the lines because things are too calm?"

Chari nodded. "Thanks for doing this. I mean, what girlfriend would ever ask her man to sleep with her sister in exchange for several thousand dollars?"

"It takes a village."

Chapter Thirteen

Riddermark's place was an old farmstead, now converted for the 21st with solar panels and water catchment systems. The main house had the original gingerbread trim and cupola. Gorgeous thing. The house had an addition built off the back end that was done in keeping with the style. The milking parlor housed a recording studio and the stock was more a petting zoo than working farm.

"Chari," Mel Riddermark said, kissing her on both cheeks. "I'm happy to host your little gathering. I've everything set up according to that thoughtful list you provided. Why, I even drew the sigils on the windows in soap. What fun! I do hope you will invite me to your temple once it's all set up."

"Of course, Mel. You'll be the first one invited."

"My boys will like that."

Chari smiled. Mel was a Hellenic priest. His Patrons were Apollon and Hermes. Though he claimed his greatest ambition was to be an Aphrodite's woman.

Mel continued. "Just make sure that those energetic little Norse gods of yours don't break my pretty things."

"This is an informal gathering to plan the ritual. All gods will be on a short leash."

"Hmmm. Well, when the day comes—please, no rips and bite marks on the upholstery."

Chari kissed Mel on the cheek. "This is just planning. I promise, no piss stains on the carpet."

"Thank you, beautiful. I'll leave you the keys, because I am going out with the girls—or rather out with the boys in drag. It's Tina Turner day at the Purple Prose downtown."

"You enjoy, my sweet. Will we see you later?" Chari asked.

"Doubtful. The boys and I get a room and continue the parade with wine and brie."

"I'll leave the keys under the mat."

Chari and Johnny walked around to the back of the grand old house. A luscious garden path led to the stone arched doorway. "Oh, my. He has certainly put in a few upgrades since I was last here."

Johnny took the key and unlocked the door. "Yes, well it must be very grand to be not only a famous local celebrity, but independently wealthy."

"Oh, this will do just fine. We can go over things today, and in two weeks, hold the ritual after Mercury is out of retrograde and Venus is high. I honestly don't see anything I'd need to improve upon for the ritual. Look at that sofa. It's already circular. No folding chairs in this house." She opened a door off the main room. "Oh, dear gods. The bathroom is a religious experience. Look at this."

Johnny slid his arm around her waist and peered over her shoulder at the dual shower and glass block and steel room. "Wanna fool around?"

"Verity should be here soon. I do not wish to be caught in *fragrante delicto* by my sister."

"Hmmm. Very well. I defer to your usual common sense and wisdom. But making love to you in that shower would be memorable."

She slapped Johnny on the rear end. "Incorrigible." Her cell phone chirped. "It's her." She began an animated conversation with Verity. "Around back. No, we've been here about fifteen minutes. Not much to set up. This place is perfect."

She hit end call just as Verity slid in the back door.

"Verity!" Chari embraced her sister. "I've missed you."

Verity deeply hugged her sister. When the embrace ended, she glanced toward Johnny. "Hi." *Oh, dear gods. He is so handsome. Look at those eyes of his. Full of mischief.*

He held out his hand. "Nice to meet you."

The twins stood together, holding hands. Though dressed differently, they were identical. *This is going to be more fun than I thought it would be.* "You two...I can barely tell you apart." *Two beautiful brown-eyed women. Identical save for the hair styles. One parts on the right, the other on the left. I wonder if they planned that. Ladies...I can take you both on. Let's retire to that magnificent shower and do each other until we are so spent we can barely walk.*

"Mother made us wear bracelets. Mine was green. Chari's was yellow. It really pissed her off when we switched."

Chari took charge. "Well, I don't see any reason we shouldn't get this show on the road. You two sit down and get acquainted. The kitchenette is in the other room. I'll go make some coffee. Give you a little privacy. Please remember, though there are wards in place, we have not cast a circle. In other words, please don't drink and drive. You get my meaning, right? Safety first."

"Thanks, babe," Johnny said, pushing an easy chair closer to the circular sectional.

Verity took Johnny's cue and pulled the other velveteen chair toward his. They would sit comfortably across from each other with a little end table between them. Probably much safer than sitting on the sofa. She looked at Johnny's physique as he sat. Much safer. *I feel as though I know him already. Intimately.*

Chari slipped through the pocket door into the kitchenette, sliding the door closed behind her.

"Nice to finally meet you. Though I kind of feel we've already met. And it's not because you and Chari are twins."

The lights flickered. *Loki is here.* She could barely breathe for the Lokean energy surrounding Johnny. "Nice to meet you, too. You know, I went through the whole thing in a dream," Verity said.

Johnny nodded. "Yep. Me, too." He began to share his dream. "I showed up at your house, completely disheveled and panicked. Loki pushing against the back of my head—you know how he does that, right? He seems to be connected to my cerebellum. Man, he wanted to ride the horse—bad. There was no ritual. No list. No personal protection. Just Loki in my body and my body in you."

"In the dream...I let you in." Verity glanced up at Johnny, feeling flushed, and a little embarrassed.

Johnny nodded. "I stepped into your house and was gone. Loki had jumped in hard. I was in the trunk. I trusted him. I knew it was coming, but I didn't feel fully prepared for that level of possession. I'm not sure I will ever feel ready for that level. But, I pulled the stick out of my ass and allowed Loki nearly full control. The trunk wasn't locked. I knew I could open it and re-emerge at any time. It's kind of a thing with me to always be in control. Former cop." Johnny paused. "I honestly wasn't sure I could do it—even in dreamland. Not because of you or anything. You are very attractive, and I, at some other time in my life, would have wanted to get to know you in a different way than how we are acquainted now. I have a strong Catholic school boy mentality. It's a problem sometimes. Monogamy and all that."

"I get it. I do. Surrender isn't easy. But this is for Chari, whom we both love—and for science."

Johnny laughed.

Verity continued sharing her dream. "In the dream, you swept me into your arms. We kissed. A long, delicious kiss. The kind of kiss that penetrates all the way to one's nether regions."

"Beyond that. It penetrated my soul. My essence. I wanted you. I needed you. He needed you. Desperately."

"I tasted Loki on your lips. I was so ready." Verity paused. "And I want to put this on the table now—I'm not actively looking. So, neither of us should get too attached—which can happen after people are intimate. I'm glad my sister has found a long-term love with whom she is making a life, but that is not for me right now. What we are going to do—it's not about good looks or shaved legs. It is an offering and a compact between spirit and mortal. In this instance to benefit *Revived Intimacy* and to support yours and my sister's dreams. And mine. I have been theoretical about this long enough. It's time for a little, excuse the phrase, hands-on experience."

Johnny nodded and smoothed his beard. "I love your sister. And I understand, completely. In the dream—we made love hard. We were drenched with sweat and the feeling of satisfaction I felt ran deeper than what can be obtained through sexual congress. It was euphoric. Divine."

Verity laughed. "Oh, yes. Indeed. Loki took control of everything, and our bodies responded accordingly."

"I know you now. Do you get that? I feel like I've been with you a hundred times. I know how you like to be kissed, how much you enjoy certain positions—one in particular," Johnny said.

Verity blushed. "Yes."

"I'm not much for saying all the right words. Chari says I don't have a romantic bone in my body. I kind of feel like I have an invitation to..."

"Put me on a sexual rotisserie?"

Johnny nodded.

"Shall we get on with Chari's list of questions?" Verity asked. "She certainly is thorough." She scrolled up and down her phone's version of the document.

Johnny stretched out in the overstuffed chair across from Verity. She glanced up as he rested one leg over an arm, taking a position that reminded her of a portrait of Loki lounging on Odin's throne.

"How formal shall we make the invitation for Loki? Light a candle and invoke his name or pour out...there's a bottle of good whiskey up on the top shelf of the bookcase behind you. What's your preference?

Verity watched as Johnny rubbed the back of his head as if he had an occipital lobe headache. Telltale sign of impending possession. *This could be interesting.* "He's already here. Please...let him speak."

Johnny leaned forward to toy with the book of matches left on the table. He flipped it open and struck the sulfur-tipped piece of cardboard to striker to produce flame. The candle wick sputtered before sparking to bright blue flicker. He watched the fire dance. He then glanced upward at Verity.

Handsome man. Graying, but in a sexy way. Blue eyes now aglow with spirit. Johnny must be in the trunk—fully possessed. Or at least he is relaxed enough to allow Loki's continence through. "Hello, Loki," she said softly.

"Surprise," he whispered. He bounded across the table, spilling the candle. Verity shrieked as Johnny's spirit-driven body pinned her in a long embrace. The over-stuffed chair rattled under their weight and movements. Verity shifted positions with Johnny and sat astride his left leg. He pulled her in for another long kiss. She instinctively moved against his thigh. She broke the kiss and nibbled his beardy chin. "I've waited for this for a long time."

"But?"

"What's the password? So help me, I will ride you to glory right here, right now, if you..."

Johnny's Loki-possessed smile grew Cheshire Cat-like. "He was mastered by the sheer surging of life, the tidal wave of being, the perfect joy of each separate muscle, joint, and sinew in that it was everything that was not death, that it was aglow and rampant, expressing itself in movement, flying exultantly under the stars." He moved his hands around her waist to her breasts. "Jack London. Call of the Wild. One of my personal favorites."

"This is not sacred space, but ritual or not..."

"My presence makes this sacred space. Rituals are for humans, not gods."

She slid onto the floor to kneel before him and pulled at Johnny's belt. He laughed—Loki's laugh—and unfastened the leather strap. She tugged the zipper down and drew his member from the boxer briefs. He was hard. She needed it. Mouth to cock. She wanted to take all of it. She inched her way to his pelvis, taking the full length and girth of his manhood into her throat as far as she could. Saliva built up at the head as she moved her lips up and down at the base. She pulled up, capturing the head and swallowing before moving her mouth to the hilt a second, third, and fourth time. Like devouring a popsicle on a hot summer day, she lavished his penis with ardor she'd never felt before. She wanted to consume him. Needed to consume him.

Johnny's hands went to her head, taking a ride on her short modified undercut hair. A low, throaty sound, a hum, ushered from his lips. Loki commanded a galdr. The song of runes. She felt the vibration of the intonation far more clearly than she heard it. Johnny must have a soulful singing voice. Loki's strength moves it into the pure and far-reaching category. The runes danced about her like puffs of smoke. She captured a rhythm in her oral congress and but moments later, she accepted Johnny's seed down her throat. Loki's semen often had a cinnamon fragrance in their astral bed. This was no different. Verity sat back on her heels. "Well, so much for Chari's list. Number two regarded fluid exchange. That ship has sailed."

Johnny laughed. Loki laughed.

So entwined were they that Verity saw only her Beloved. Her Patron. Old Flame Hair. He was as delicious as the morning's first cup of coffee or nibble of chocolate on a bad day.

He stroked her head like petting a kitty. "Your mouth is amazing."

Verity stood and ripped off her clothes. No need to be a seductress, stripper, or vixen. This was a sure thing. I could wear galoshes and a bag over my head and still get banged. Though she wasn't thin, by any means, being more of a moderate plus size, smaller breasts, round belly and rear-end, she didn't have qualms with showing her body. She had some meat on her bones. And she didn't care. Johnny's body had a sweet little pooch and barrel chest. He had slim hips. Nice shoulder definition and upper arms. It was the fire in his eyes that sent her over the moon. That and the profound tumescence.

He reached out for her. "I have waited a long time for this."

"We're being naughty," Verity replied, snuggling into his chest.

"We are, but not too naughty. This is sacred space, and Chari did not exactly specify by contract the venue for our congress. She planned the date and place without vetting it. So, I say—this is our ritual. This is where you learn the magic of sacred sex and I gain my heart's desire."

She kissed his pectoral muscles. "I'm sure I warned her to never leave anything to chance with Loki."

He caressed her back and kissed her throat. "True that." He slid two fingers between her legs to knead her clitoris. He slipped his middle finger inside her. "You're ready for me."

"I've been ready for years."

"Shall we prolong this sweet agony by continuing foreplay, or shall I fill you deeply, right now, let us reach a state of bliss together, then go back and do all the things in round two? My mouth aches to taste your quim—but I sense that you need me in you. Right now."

Verity flushed as she deliberately stared into his eyes. They were freakishly blue. Blue with flickering flame behind them. She looked at his mouth, surrounded by that sweet Van Dyke beard. It invited her to nibble. "I want you—now."

"Very well, then." He dropped to the floor and positioned himself atop her. He thrust his hips and the head of his cock found her entrance easily. She was so slick with need her body was like a homing beacon for his great ship. Verity raised her hips to meet his first thrust.

He moved in her, against her. Each pass of his shaft drew her clitoris from its hood and a brilliant flood of orgasm began to build. She pressed her pelvis toward him, meeting his thrusts, trying to rub her clit against his pubic bone. She couldn't help but moan. She wasn't sure she could keep quiet. *Fuck it. This is not a time to be demure. I am fucking a god!*

Their physical coupling became astral as she left her body in the throes of orgasm. Within the explosion of orgasm another sensation emerged, strong and bright. Cosmic and brilliant. It rode the wave of her climax and accelerated her pleasure. It was unlike any other experience. Even as she came, the educator came forth. Always an academic. *No one has experienced this for a thousand years. This is the pure pleasure of creation. That infinite spark of life.* From what must have been the vault of heaven, she witnessed the god-touched Johnny and her own willing and accepting body make love.

A pulsating warmth coursed through her from toes to crown, centering deep inside her body. Instead of the "Oh, fuck" associated with so many sexual contacts born of youthful passion sans protection, she took a breath and relaxed into the moment. When the last vestige of pleasure had escaped her, she felt the pull to return. Return to her body. Return to the mundane reality—as if anything could ever truly be mundane with Loki as patron. As she literally came down from the high, she felt momentarily, and very suddenly, empty. *It's already gone. Conceived and given flight. How do I feel about this? I am both in a state of jubilee and sorrow. Gebo can be harsh. This is one I am going to need to consider later. In depth.*

She whispered, seeing the sparkle of godhood still in Johnny's eyes. "Wow. Just wow."

He pulled away, his member finally at rest. "Well, how did you enjoy empirical research?"

"There are no words." Verity rested her arm against her forehead. "We seem to be ignoring Chari's list of rules—which I had always thought was a given in these instances. Instead, I didn't care how you took me, as long as you did."

"I love her, but this is truly a let go and let god moment. I find it's best just to not take her outbursts personally and move on to the next job. So to speak." He paused. "Our health histories have been vetted. And though we did not glove up, Chari told me you have an IUD. Something about the ten-year plan for birth control. This was about his needs. We made a cake—and ritual is icing to him. It's really to feed his ego. He says all space is sacred in his presence. She has nothing to complain about."

Verity didn't want to put a damper on the moment by sharing that she had conceived and given up to the gods, a child, all in the same moment. A Nephilim. Would Johnny even understand? No. This remains secret.

"So," Johnny began, scrambling for his pants. "Was it good for you?"

"Good? Ummm...amazing. It was amazing. I stand amazed. I like this hands-on experience thing. I've been feeding my brain for decades but have ignored my flesh." She paused. "Where the hell is my bra?"

"He'll be back, you know." Johnny tossed Verity's black sports bra to her.

"I know. He's never far."

Verity picked herself up and took to her chair. "That was incredible. Would you mind if I made a few notes?"

Johnny laughed. "Charity told me you were mostly business. Lost in academia, I believe she said."

"And she collects salt shakers. So what?"

"Oh, dear. That struck a nerve. Have you and Chari been on opposite sides of the creative spectrum since being in-utero?"

"Yep. We're not identical twins."

Johnny pulled himself into his chair and dressed. "I need to ground. I cannot feel my hands and feet." He lifted his chin and called out, "Chari! Coffee! Please!"

Damn. He is good-looking. "She's going to figure it out. I smell like sex. We smell like sex."

"I need water, protein, and something like a rock or pile of dirt." Then softly to Verity,

"Loki jumped in hard and jumped out harder. This is what I get for giving him control, huh? A headache."

Chari called from beyond the door as she slid it open. "What is it, babe? Did my sister put you in a choke hold? She's been known to do that."

Verity rubbed her temples. "Stop it, sis. No teasing."

Chari set a tray of coffees and cookies on the table. "All right...this room is in a state of disarray. I knew I should have stayed to monitor things."

Johnny reached out for her. "Babe, Loki jumped in. I need to ground. Can you get me something to hold? A rock. A fucking brick. Something into which I can transfer the excess energy?"

"You're supposed to make the rules for that. You are in control of spirit possession—not the spirits."

Johnny sighed. "Babe, please. No lectures on drawing down the spirits right now. It is what it is. I allowed it. It was a hard ride." He reached for the honey bear and squeezed a goodly amount into his coffee followed by heavy cream.

"All right. All right. I'm sorry. I'm glad Loki dropped by—but remind him that his vessels are fragile." Chari darted from the room.

Verity poured cream into a coffee and then lifted it to her lips. "She knows. I think she'll be okay with it—except she didn't get to be in control of the situation. The ritual."

"She does like her rituals."

"As much as I enjoy research."

"Verity," Johnny began. "I would not find it objectionable to horse Loki again—you know—purely for scientific documentation." He winked.

"Well, for the sake of empirical research, I think comparison is always appropriate. We can see if we can reproduce the same or similar results."

"I feel a paper in your future."

"Fuck. I feel an entire novel."

Chapter Fourteen

Chari pulled up a side chair and fixed her coffee. She scooted an extremely large piece of obsidian toward Johnny. "Mel has quite the collection of minerals. I don't think he'll mind us borrowing this one. Ground, baby." She turned to her sister. "So? Did the three of you come to an accord?"

Verity nodded. "Well, we came. There was coming. Yes."

Chari fell back into the chair, crestfallen. "You fucked Loki, didn't you?" She paused. "No wonder I had trouble getting things to work in the kitchen. Everything was just off. First the light switch, then the coffeemaker. Then I dropped the works and had to start again. Loki. Fuck."

Verity nodded. "Sorry not sorry. Look, Charity, it wasn't planned. You know Loki is the god of spontaneity."

"This is entirely premature." Chari crossed her arms in front of her. Her vibe was seriously closed off. "I calculated the best day and time."

Verity looked at Johnny. "Nothing was premature."

He sniggered.

"All right, you are not going to take this seriously, are you? I should have known the two of you—excuse me—three of you, wouldn't be able to control yourselves."

"Now, Charity, don't take that tone with me. The entire point of this congress was for me to make love with my patron in exchange for the closing costs. And dearest sister, there are no words of gratitude grand enough to express the...fuck. I just want to scream *eureka*. I now get what all the fuss was about."

"Lifted you right out of academia. Jeez. I've been trying to do that for years. But I kind of had my heart set on the whole process."

"Just because it will not be our maiden voyage does not mean we cannot sail the good ship Loki into port a second time," Johnny said.

Charity held up her hand. "Let's not use nautical metaphors about spirit-driven sex, shall we?"

Verity laughed. "Oh, please. Let's. I can think of so many good metaphors." She stopped short as Chari gave her a look that could have turned ice cold.

"So, what have we learned here today, sisters? That I am far more open-headed than I thought. That Verity now has the practical experience needed to add a touch of realism to her lessons. And Charity, well, you're seeing your dreams come to pass. And I'm going to be there with you every step of the way."

Chari lifted herself from the edge of Verity's chair, reached out, and kissed Johnny lightly. "Running it alone until you can get out of your contract will be a pain in the ass. I won't be able to start up the lunch service."

"What?" Verity interjected. "What do you mean?"

Johnny palmed the obsidian like it was a baseball. "I signed a non-compete. My employer wants a fuck-ton of money for me to buy my way out of it. It won't stop my move, but it will slow it way down. And knowing that I plan on leaving will not make my employer behave any more decently than a viper trapped in a jar."

Chari touched Johnny's leg. "Even after we get the money for the antiques we sell and cash in our retirements we still won't have quite enough for him just to walk away."

"I'm tapped, sis. I can't afford any more right now. In six months, probably."

"I'm not going to ask you for money. Is that not a scenario we learned not to explore as children?"

Verity nodded. "Don't touch my piggy bank."

Chari held up her hand to display a thin scar across her knuckles.

Verity shrugged. "I hit her with my scissors. I hadn't expected her to get sliced open."

"You are overlooking the obvious," Johnny said softly. He reclined and put one leg over the armrest.

The air pressure in the room changed. It grew thick and heavy like a warm fog. The lights flickered. Chari sighed. "Oh, look. It's my handsome lover possessed by a creepy god—who doesn't knock."

"Quick witted to the end. And I have permission. We discussed it, as this conversation was starting to bore me. Worry, worry, worry. Is that all you twenty-first century mortals do?"

"We live in society and are subject to its conventions, Loki." Verity felt her face flush. "It's nice to see you again so soon."

Johnny leaped like a cat onto the seat of his chair, perching on the bottom cushion with both feet. "What do you teach about me, Verity?"

"Well, all lessons boil down to the fact that you offer the problem in one hand and the solution in the other. It's up to us to choose."

"All this fuss over money does not slake my thirst. I am not satiated. Have either of you thought about asking me for help? I can be useful out of the realm of a conjugal visit as much as I am in one."

Chari shook her head. "Ask you directly to intervene with Johnny's boss? To soften pharos hard heart so he will set his slave free?"

"A rose by any other name, dear." Johnny stood abruptly. "Well, I'm hungry. Johnny is hungry. I don't often get an opportunity to dine with such lovely women. Perhaps a little glass of wine will loosen you up. Or, you could just ask."

Chari stood and slid her arms around Johnny's neck. "I'm asking, Loki. Will you help us?" She pecked him on the lips.

"Of course I will help. It's not hard to set such things in motion. In fact, I have already done so." He paused. "This vessel needs to ground. It's like being seasick while making passage in the hold of a ship. Where is that black glass?" Johnny looked at his hands. "Oh, dear. I'm holding it. Yes. He needs to ground."

Johnny reached out and pulled Verity in tightly, so both sisters were in his arms.

"Excuse me a moment. I don't mean to leave the presence of a god, but I have something in the toaster oven. And if I don't get it now, it won't be the only thing burning."

Chari stepped into the kitchenette—this time leaving the door ajar.

"What do you want, Loki?" She caressed his clean-shaven cheek with hers. She thought of a cat rubbing up against a willing hand.

"More."

Their lips met. A long, slow, intimate kiss. Verity lost herself in the embrace. She gave up fear, guilt, societal pressure. Johnny's body. Loki's spirit.

When they parted, Verity giggled. "It's a good thing Charity isn't greedy or selfish *this* way."

"Even if not horsed, she and Johnny have understandings regarding such things. There is nothing you can do to him that would bother her. He is a little more hesitant, but overall, he would succumb to your touch and find pleasure with you. In you."

"I think I just came a little."

"Of course you did."

Charity re-entered the room. "Oh, dear gods. Can you two separate at all?"

"Yes, we can." Verity pulled away, but Johnny held fast. "Loki...it's time to go."

"Yes. I need to leave. His body temperature is rising." Loki sat and began the process of exiting stage left—relieving the horse of rider. Eyes closed, breaths slow and steady, Johnny returned. He stood and shook off the excess energy like a dog out of water. "Holy shit."

Verity giggled. "I hope you're not saying that about the quality of our embrace."

"No. That was great. He really loves you."

"How do you feel, honey?" Charity asked.

"Like a million dollars. Confident." He paused. "Are we allowed to raid Mel's kitchen or is there a buffet somewhere around here?"

"We haven't really gone over all the details yet." Chari had such a perturbed look on her face that Verity laughed.

"I think that ship has sailed. I feel comfortable with my experience and am happy to cut *Revived Intimacy* a check.

"Do you think you might need a follow up? Strictly for science, of course," Johnny asked.

Verity looked into his nebulae blue eyes. "Indeed."

On their way to the car Johnny leaned into Verity, and whispered, "He has a surprise for you."

Verity chuckled. "More?"

Johnny nodded. "Oh yes. Much more."

"I can hardly wait," she replied.

Chapter Fifteen

Verity wasn't sure she could possibly retain anything her sister said over dinner. She watched Johnny and Chari. They were good together. Obviously in love. They weren't gregarious in their public affections, but she knew they had hands clasped under the table. She had to shake off a slight twinge of jealousy. It wasn't Johnny that she craved. It was Loki. He is hunger. He is desire. He offers the ability to overcome deluded impulses by pushing them into your face and making you choose. She swallowed her desires and attempted at a level that rested in her very core, to not look at Johnny as if he were the living embodiment of her divine spouse. Though he was wildly attractive, he was not hers. And then Johnny looked up from his plate and flashed sly blue eyes baring the sparkle of the heavens. Loki.

Verity took the saucer from under her mug and slid a dumpling onto it. She set it aside. "God plate," she said. Johnny and Chari nodded. "I believe Loki enjoys Chinese dumplings as much as the next god."

"He likes it," Johnny said softly.

"Is he chatty?" Verity asked. She could tell by the glimmer in Johnny's eyes that he was not alone. *He is definitely horsed—but at a level where both occupied the same space. Maybe a 70% Johnny, 30% Loki split. Aspecting. He's aspecting—aware of everything yet sharing space with spirit.*

"He's pretty pleased with himself."

His foot brushed hers from across the table. Verity smiled slightly. Inward, she quashed excitement so rich she could taste it.

"Well, how about I call the bank and transfer the funds into your account, sister?" *How's about I offer another grand to sleep with your boyfriend again.*

"Wow. Yes, please." Chari teared up as her sister poked at her smart phone's banking app to transfer funds.

Verity looked up from her screen for a moment. Johnny and Chari were in each other's arms. A loud ping broke their embrace. Johnny pulled his cell phone from his shirt pocket. He read the message, then fell back against his chair. "Holy sht."

Chari touched his arm lightly. "What is it?"

"Asshat accepted $5000.00 to let me out of my contract." He paused. "Chari, I'm moving!" He kissed Chari quickly, then rose and went around the table. He pulled Verity into his arms. "Thank you. Thank you. Thank you."

Verity felt suddenly awkward. "My pleasure."

She and Johnny giggled like school children and hugged again.

Chari took a sip of her wine. "Well...I guess formal ritual was not needed, after all. The gods have certainly made their point."

"There's plenty of time for more formal rituals, sis. You know that the Norse gods aren't big on formalities. You should host a blot in their honor after the restaurant opens. Kind of an after-hours boast and toast."

"I will. Great idea. You will come, yes?"

"And my brother, too. I'll get him to clear his schedule a little," Johnny said.

"You have a brother?" Verity asked.

"With his own plane," Chari replied.

"Oh my. Is he a pilot?" Verity asked.

"He works the university lecture circuit. Good money."

Verity's interest piqued. "And of what does he lecture?"

"Oh, you'll like this. He lectures on the history of the Catholic Church as it intertwines with Santeria and Christo-paganism. And more. He's interesting."

"I bet he is. I look forward to meeting him."

Johnny winked. Verity blushed.

VERITY SLIPPED IN THE back door of The Stew restaurant and wandered into the dining area. *Oh, sweet. Johnny is here.* She took note of the headphones and laptop before him. *He's on a break or something.* She crept up behind him and slipped her arms around his shoulders. "Hi, handsome."

He pulled out his earplugs and turned in his chair then rose. "Well, hello to you, too."

Verity planted a kiss square on his mouth, lingering a moment before pulling away. She placed her head on his shoulder and gave him a squeeze. "Sexy as always, I see." He returned the hug and moved a hand affectionately to the small of her back. She whispered into his ear, "I know I shouldn't say this, but I've missed you."

And then she looked up to see Johnny smiling at her from the door to the kitchen. "Hi Ver. Can I get you a cup of coffee—if you're finished molesting my brother, that is."

Verity panicked and backed away. "You're not Johnny." She calmed her flight mode. "I'm sorry."

"I'm Jack. I'm not sure, but I believe you are Charity's twin, since she does not yet greet me with kisses."

She felt herself flush from crown to toes. "Yes. I'm sorry. I'm Verity."

Jack still had hands on her waist. "Nice to meet you." He hugged her.

The overall sense of warmth that cascaded through her body at that moment was indescribable. And she tried. It was one of those things she'd want to capture in her notes. First and foremost, she was an educator, author, and secondly...no. There was no secondly.

"You are Johnny's...twin?"

Jack laughed. "Yes, as much as you are Chari's twin."

She took a step back from Jack and cast a hard glance at Johnny. "You never told me you were a twin."

"It did not seem germane to our activities." He smirked. "I'm glad you're here."

Verity smiled, still feeling the heat of embarrassment rouge her cheeks. "I wouldn't miss the first official dinner and ritual of *Revived Intimacy*. I even paid my two hundred and sixty bucks."

"You would have been free. Now, Jack here...I made him pay double."

"Johnny, you didn't tell me Chari's sister was so lovely," Jack said.

"I told you they were identical twins."

Jack released Verity's waist and put his hands on his hips. "Well, I bet everyone else believes they are identical. I doubt they are. Verity, you have a lot of energy coming off you. You brighten a room."

Verity giggled. "Well, aren't you a gentleman."

"I'm no gentleman. I wonder...is your glow divine in origin? I think the energy is far more godly. Hermes? No...Loki."

"Holy shit, Jack." Verity's puzzled expression made Johnny chuckle. He moved to stand shoulder to shoulder with his twin. "Yes. My brother, though not active in the community, is quite gifted."

Verity studied the identical faces. Clean shaven, except for well-trimmed Van Dyke, graying hair, freakishly blue eyes, and friendly first impression.

"Where are you staying, Verity?" Jack asked.

"Airbnb in town. She calls it a hobbit house."

"A round cottage with an artificial thatch roof with two adjoining rooms and a jacuzzi on the patio in the back? How lovely. I'm staying in the other room. How about we open the door in between our rooms tonight and have a slumber party?"

Johnny slapped his brother on the back. "Don't scare her off, Jack."

"You don't need to protect me, Johnny. But thanks."

Take a chance on flirting? "I'll keep the door open."

"I'll bring a nice red. Say, about ten o'clock? Or we could relax in the hot tub. Did you bring your swim suit?"

Verity looked up through her thick eyelashes. "I did not. But don't let that stop you.

"Funny, I forgot mine, too."

Verity felt confident. "Sit with me during dinner?"

Jack smiled. "I wouldn't sit anywhere else now that I've met you."

Verity addressed Johnny. "What have you got to eat around this place?"

"Shall I get you a cheese and cracker tray and a cabernet from the bar so you and my brother can have a little two-person mixer?" Johnny asked.

"That sounds good, John." He held his elbow out to Verity. "Join me on the patio, madam? Oh, and how about a carafe of coffee?"

Verity took his arm and they strolled away.

"Oh, don't mind me! I've just got a five-course dinner buffet for seventeen to cook."

"Thanks, Johnny. Be sure to bring us clean mugs." Jack didn't look back as he ribbed his brother.

Johnny hung his head and took a deep breath. He exhaled and headed into his kitchen to prepare a snack for his brother and Verity. He thought about what he was doing. *For my brother and Verity. I wonder...*

Jack and Verity settled in to a glass-top patio table under a forest-green canopy. Jack scooted his chair closer to hers. "I'd like to see the view."

"Oh, yes. The grounds are lovely," Verity replied.

"Yes, you are." He reached out to hold her hand. "Please forgive my being so forward. I feel compelled."

"Well, that's a great pick-up line."

He laughed. "I feel as though we have been moved into position by the hands of the gods. I've always thought myself their rook, and never a pawn. And you...you are their queen."

"I am so not regal," Verity replied. She allowed Jack's hand to intertwine with hers. "But, this," she held up their locked hands, "is nice."

"I think what John and Charity have accomplished here is pretty amazing. From inception to this very moment, and with all the moving and shaking in between, they're making their dreams come true." He paused. "What are your dreams, Verity?"

She choked on her own spit. "My dreams?"

"Sure. Your dreams."

"Well, I sold my first piece of fiction—a mystical romance—and I'd like to get through the first round of edits without too much more bloodshed."

"You know what they say. Good edits make a good book."

"True that. My agent is already pushing it out to screenwriters and producers."

"Big." He squeezed her hand.

Verity replied, "Very big."

"Tell me the plot. Every detail."

"You read romance novels?" she asked.

"I have. I read everything. The truth is, that I'd like to feel that kind of love again. The love where nothing else matters, except the sound of her breath in the night. The flash of her smile in the sun. Her face beaming during climax. It's been a very long time since I've trusted anyone deep enough to say the words."

"I love you?"

"No, not that. Tell someone my middle name. it's scary. My parents are freaks."

Verity caught the smirk on Jack's face and knew he was teasing.

"Well, it's London. My name is Jack London Lightman. I'd tell you Johnny's, but he'd probably go from salty to stabby pretty quick."

Verity consciously closed her mouth as she realized her jaw was agape. "Jack London?"

"Yep."

Johnny kicked open the door and placed a tray of coffee and snacks on the patio table. "Do not, under any circumstances, tell her my full name. Brother? Do you hear me?"

"I cannot guarantee that, Johnny." Jack poured two coffees.

"Fuck you. Verity, this is a preemptive strike. My name is John Steinbeck Lightman."

"Your secret is safe with me," Verity replied.

"Our parents are librarians. I'm certain we were conceived in some clandestine fashion in the stacks of old National Geographic magazines. Our names, at least, are not as bad as our sister's," Jack said.

Johnny interjected. "Dolly Levi. And she has red hair."

Verity looked at Jack, puzzled.

"*Hello Dolly*. Not a book, but a musical. It played at a drive-in right before our parents wed. We've never asked, but we've done the math and we think our sister may have been conceived that night."

"Well, now that all the family skeletons are out of the closet, whatever shall we speak of at dinner?" Verity laughed and squeezed Jack's hand. "My favorite author is Jack London, so I get it." *And if I am misreading signs and wonders of the gods, then strike me down now. Holy crap. Thank you, Loki. Is this your way of saying "thanks?"*

"I'm going to get the chickens in now. My support staff doesn't arrive for another hour. You two are always welcome to come in and lend a hand," Johnny said.

"Go away, little brother. Verity and I are enjoying our coffees."

Verity turned to Jack as Johnny headed back into his kitchen. "We should probably help. Your brother. My sister. Isn't that what family is for? To help?"

"They are both control freaks, and I learned a long time ago to stay the hell away when he's working. Trust me. We are far safer out here. Grape?" He passed the snack tray to Verity.

"Yeah. Yes. Charity is sequestered, working out last-minute details of the ritual, so, yes. I'm sure this will be a production beyond compare."

"Right. So, it is prudent of us to stay away and out of their way until we are called for dinner. But not from each other." Jack paused. "Verity, would you please hide with me—here at The Stew restaurant?"

"I am happy to stay right here with you. Though I was going to run back to my Airbnb to change before dinner."

"Me, too. Let's go. I took Uber here. You have something that seats more than one?"

"I do." Verity took her cell phone from her purse and texted her sister. *Going with Jack back to the Airbnb to change. See you soon?*

Chapter Sixteen

"I think I'm hungry," Verity said as she pulled out of the parking lot and down the tree-lined driveway to the interstate. The pit of her stomach had a dull tickle and her palms were sweating.

"I thought I was hungry, too—but I believe it's something else. Verity, although we've only just met, I believe I am infatuated. I find you quite appealing."

Yeah...and I slept with your brother when he was wearing a god. "Feeling is mutual."

The hobbit house wasn't far. Verity stopped the car and sat hands-on-wheel, eyes downcast for a moment.

"Are you all right?" Jack asked.

"I'm thirty-seven years old. I think I'm old enough to both control my baser instincts and act upon them."

"I'm forty-eight and have lived my life pretty much by-the-book. Straight laced. A tad bit stoic. But here I sit, my belly full of butterflies for the first time in a decade and I'm really not in the mood to play by societal rules I had no hand in creating."

"Yep." Verity paused for a moment. She gave a sideways glance to Jack. "Wrong or right, I think we should head inside." She slapped his thigh. "I'll buy you dinner later, huh?"

Jack laughed. "I think this is the start of a beautiful friendship."

Verity turned the key to her little cottage. "With benefits."

Once inside, Jack pulled her into his arms. "I'm going to kiss you now. I'm going to touch you and make love to you."

Not to be outdone, Verity ran her right hand across Jack's chest and down to his belt. "And I'm going to allow all of it." She unfasted his buckled. "Chari would be pleased that we've discussed consent."

Jack slid his hands up her t-shirt and cupped her breasts over her bra. "You are exactly what I have been waiting for."

"A woman with good lingerie?"

They both fought back laugher as they kissed. Surely, it was the most joyous embrace of either of their lives.

Verity wanted to release control and let Jack have his way with her. She felt the surge of orgasm well within her more times than she could count as their kisses grew more daring and explorative. *I cannot come in the air. I cannot come in the air. What am I supposed to do? Think of the queen?* She heard Loki chuckle, low and hot. *You are supposed to climax. Nothing else. Enjoy it. So help me, beloved, if you start thinking of anything but his mouth against your swollen clitoris, I will take back my little present.*

She wanted to close her mind to Loki. *Get out of my head because I am going to...*

Scream. She wrapped her fingers around the crown of Jack's salt and pepper head and emitted a loud, long, guttural cry that harkened back to the first orgasm given by a man to a woman and rode the currents of time from climax to climax to that moment. She held his face against her quim and writhed.

LIKE A TROOPER JACK allowed the manhandling as he gently flicked his tongue against her and tasted the crowning glory of his ministrations. *I haven't had it this good in years. Oh, sweet Verity—let's not ever get out of this bed.*

He pulled back and up onto his knees, his thick cock in his hand. "Verity...I don't have a condom."

"How long has it been since you had intercourse?" she asked.

"Truthfully? About four years. This lady I was seeing—it ended badly when she wanted to play with handcuffs and hot wax. Not my thing. But we always used condoms."

"And I have never had unprotected sex, last time currently not recalled due to the loss of blood flow to my brain—thank you very much." She strained to reach for the nightstand drawer. "But, safety first. Look what the hobbits left us." She pulled out a three-pack of condoms. "And there is lube and some kind of honey dust shit."

"Just hand me that condom."

"Hmmm. Thirty seconds of conversation did not deflate that magnificent erection at all." Verity laid back and opened herself to him.

He obliged. Thoroughly. Deeply.

Verity realized immediately that this man had some serious skill at thrusting. He made certain each push in rubbed the apex of her pussy, drawing her clit out of its sheathe. The condom had those little ridges on it and felt stimulating, not uneventful.

She smelled his perspiration and heard his breathing become shallow. He had a sexy body for a middle-aged man, and she gripped his slim hips as he thrust. He scrunched his face as he came—something she barely noticed as she, too, orgasmed.

Spent, he rested atop her.

"We came at the same time. How awesome is that?"

"I don't recall ever having had that happen before." He pulled away and found a waste basket for the used condom. He stopped to peer into the open drawer as he slid back into bed. "Man, I love those hobbits. Like Boy Scouts. Always prepared."

"What time is it?" she asked. Her cell phone chirped. She answered her own question as she took up her phone to read the text message. "We have a little over an hour, Jack. I say soak in the Jacuzzi, because if I order pizza my sister will kill me."

"Is that Chari?"

Verity nodded and replied to the message. *We came back to our rooms to change.*

Jack laughed. "One. Two. Three—"

Verity's phone rang.

"I called that," Jack said.

"Hello, Charity," Verity said, trying to control her still-heavy breaths.

"I was meditating. Preparing to priestess at ritual. And I saw you. I saw you, Ver. I saw you—with Johnny. Then I realized it wasn't Johnny. It's Jack. You took Jack back to your room and fucked him."

"Yes, sis. We'll be there in time. Just taking a soak in the hot tub. Love you. See you soon." Verity ended the call and turned her ringer off. "Come on, Jack. Let's go see if we can turn into prunes. I have a crinkly broomstick skirt for tonight. My body will totally match."

They walked proudly and nude, outside into the back where the steaming hot tub awaited them. The grounds were small but manicured. There was a bamboo privacy trellis between the two rooms and another blocking the trail to the road.

Jack climbed into the tub and uttered a contented sigh as he slipped into the steam and bubbles. "Oh, baby. Get in. The water is fine."

Once in the tub, Verity cuddled up to Jack. He put his strong arm around her shoulders. "I liked that, Jack. Thank you."

"You make it sound like we swiped right and are but two ships passing in the night."

"We don't even live in the same state."

"Actually, I'm working at the University of Washington on a nine-month project. Starts next week. The university is giving me a serviced condo—meaning I don't have to clean it—and paying for a hangar for my plane at Boeing field. I'm going to train fledgling archeologists in Biblical lore so that they don't all start wearing wide-brimmed fedoras and cracking whips around the square."

Verity silenced a shudder at the words nine months. She didn't know if Loki's child had been pulled into the heavens yet. She certainly hadn't felt anything untoward.

"I made a joke."

"I'm sorry. I got it—I was just taken in by the fact that I live two hours south."

"Really?"

"I do."

He leaned over and kissed her. "I'm working Tuesday through Thursday, ten o'clock in the morning until 4:00 in the afternoon. No field work. All lecture hall."

Verity giggled. "I work Tuesday through Thursday, eight o'clock in the morning to six."

"Can I invite myself up for long weekends?"

"When you say serviced condo, what does that mean?"

"That I don't have to clean or do laundry and have executive dining room privileges, from which I can call out to dine in or hob-knob with the other visiting professors. From what I understand the undergrads who do the room service actually trained with a professional gentleman's gentleman."

"Sounds like I should take long weekends with you."

"Well, if we're together, I'm good."

Verity reached into the bubbles to stroke his cock. "I think we should get together right now." She bit his nipple. "Right. Now."

"I didn't bring a condom out here."

Verity pouted. "There are two left. One of them should go to dinner with us and the other can wait on my pillow." She released his hardness. "See you later, big guy."

"I'm sure you can coax him to make another appearance. Incidentally, how formal is this dinner?"

"Shirt and tie." Verity climbed out of the hot tub. "Panties, optional."

Chapter Seventeen

Their return to the restaurant was met with questioning faces. Chari's perhaps a bit more so than Johnny's. Verity smirked at her sister as they pushed through into the restaurant. In the time they'd been gone, Johnny's staff had set up the buffet and the staircase leading to the temple—as Chari was calling it for the evening—had literally been festooned with branches, swags, fresh flowers, and delicate gauze fabric. Verity looked up the staircase and marveled at her sister's handiwork. From the first step to the double doors at the top leading into the space claimed by *Revived Intimacy* was absolutely gorgeous. "Dear gods, Charity. I had no idea a stairwell could be so beautiful."

"Thank you, sis. My initiate will guide my guests up the staircase and secure the promise of entrance from each attendee. This is going to be a glorious evening."

"After choice of starter, entrée, salad, fresh-baked bread, sauces, cheese plate, dessert, and coffee, it will be a wonder if anyone will be able to rise from their seat much less climb that stair," Johnny said. He had changed into his chef's whites. Verity sized him up. He did look good. Very good. She cast her glance at Jack. Though dressed simply in jeans and a dress shirt with tie, he looked even better.

One of the green-aproned restaurant workers approached Johnny. "I'm going to set up the pickled vegetables and rye bread tray near the front door. Let your guests help themselves while they wait for you to open the buffet."

"Thank you," Johnny replied. "Nice to see you returned my brother in one piece. The tension was palpable when you skipped out."

Verity kissed Johnny on the cheek. "I like your brother."

Johnny glanced at Chari, who stood behind Jack and withheld a laugh as she made a closed fist victory motion and mouthing the word, "Yes."

"Let's go sit down, Verity. I see name tags and I need to rearrange them if I don't like where my brother placed me," Jack said. He boldly took Verity by the hand and led her to the first banquet table, then the second. "Oh, this will never do. We don't want to be in the first group of twelve. Let's pick our own table. In the back."

"You are bad, Jack Lightman. My sister runs on choreographed daily movements. A place for everything and everything in its place—including me."

"She'll get over it."

He took their place settings and little tent cards to a table to the far right of the dining area. "There. Put the naughty kids in the corner."

"Well, at least our conversation won't disturb others, though I think mixing is a part of the whole plan." Verity put her sweater over her chair. "Ah, and the first non-family attendees arrive."

From her position in the far right of the dining area, Verity watched her sister bounce from guest to guest, greeting each one with a hug and a kiss-kiss. *She better greet them, since dinner is $60.00 and the ritual is $200.00. How the hell did she get seventeen participants? Good for her.*

"So, what's going to happen this evening?" Jack asked.

"I think it will be a dedication and ceremony to welcome all gods and spirits to the temple and ask for their blessings for the restaurant. I don't know. She might be concentrating on the big-name deities this time. You know...Odin, Loki, Apollo, Hermes—who is really big since communication is now instantaneous. A mixed bag of gods and spirits."

Jack laughed. "Will she invite any saints? I could recommend a handful who fit what they're doing here. She should invoke St. Anthony of the Abbott. He is patron saint of bacon. And St. Drogo—he's the saint of coffee—and ugly people."

"I think, since one of her prime objectives is to get people over their hang-ups and barriers to self-love and love of others, and communion with the gods, that the majority of rituals and spirit encounters will be with those gods who are into that kind of thing."

"Well, that would certainly be Loki. In fact, he would be able to take over for all the others if need be."

Verity realized she and Jack had not yet discussed religious preferences. In fact, they had not really discussed much of anything. "I am very familiar with Loki."

"I know. Johnny told me."

Verity froze. "Oh?"

"He helped you with some research, right?"

She nodded.

Jack leaned in and whispered, "That's all that needs to be said. Ever. I don't care about any Lokean encounters of more amorous nature you may have had."

"I've had one. Exactly one. And what I learned from that single instance became the key to unlocking one hell of a novel."

"Yes. Which you have contracted—"

"With an advance."

"Congratulations, indeed. I can't wait to read it. Or perhaps I can experience some of it firsthand, no?"

Verity giggled. "I decided to write my sacred sexuality adventure as a work of fiction—as I just could not write it in precise linear fashion. Loki doesn't follow straight lines."

"He's interesting. I like the symbolism behind his lore. I've seen Johnny draw him down. Very interesting. Indeed."

"You are so...academic."

"I trust that is a good thing," Jack replied.

"It is very good."

The dinner was silent. That's how good the food was. Johnny could cook. When twenty people quit conversing to eat—you know it is seriously slow food. Delicious food. And dessert...Verity thought she might climax just looking at the delicate pastries. Profiteroles. Handmade chocolates. Sweets made from fruit and nuts. "I want to fill my purse and eat these things later."

Jack shook his head. "I already asked for a little box to take back to the hobbit house. Two of each item, plus some of the breads and cheeses for breakfast. The coffee at the house isn't bad."

"I love coffee."

"More than most things. Yes."

Verity looked around for her sister. Her focus had either been on the food or Jack. Which had more flavor? The garlic mash or Jack's kisses? *Let this be the real deal. Let this be the real deal.* The mantra rang through her head. *Jack is perfect.*

Of course he is. You asked to be fulfilled in love and marriage—not in so many words, but I know your heart, beloved. You want the drama of a mortal relationship and I handpicked a man I thought you might be able to love, and who would love you in return. Loki's voice warmed her. She listened as she cut her first dessert with her fork. *For the child you gave me, I give you as many as your heart desires. Jack is potent. You are ripe. I foresee immediate offspring.*

"Loki—what happened to the Nephilim? I'm still kind of in denial about giving up the product of conception to the gods."

Product of conception? The product of god and mortal is far greater an evolved being than the offspring of humankind. Do not have regrets or feel guilt. This was not a baby such as you know it. And if I can put your heart to rest, the child is growing as befits a divine being, surrounded by love.

"Will it know of me?"

Eventually.

"Thank you, Loki."

You're welcome. Enjoy your mortal drama.

She turned to Jack. "Where is Charity?"

"She retired to her temple. You kind of went away for a second there. God-touched a little?"

She placed her hand atop Jack's. "Jack?" she began.

"Yes?"

"Let's take a walk."

Jack rose and extended his hand to Verity. "There's a tree dedicated to Hecate somewhere around here. Tall maple with a long chain attached for folks to attach mementoes. Keys and such. Let's go find it."

Verity felt all eyes were upon them as they strolled out of the dining area and onto the grounds. "We may miss some of the ritual."

"Let's make our own." Jack slipped an arm around her waist and gave her a squeeze before taking her hand.

They walked to the tree line and then into the wooded area completely surrounding the restaurant.

"It's a bit chilly. My nipples are hard." Verity felt comfortable. "But look at that sunset."

Jack didn't reply. She pressed into him for warmth. Her breasts caressed his upper arm. His perfect height made it possible for her to press against him without awkwardness. Any taller or shorter and it wouldn't have been the same.

The tree wasn't too far off their path. A tall ladder had been erected against a huge maple and a long chain swayed from its own weight from the top branches. "Well, that is a nice tree with a nice chain. Seriously nice ladder," Jack said.

"Only the best for her gods. Chari is a spare-no-expense kind of gal."

She felt an unsubtle, deliberate touch of her left breast by Jack's upper arm. She looked up and saw something in his smirk that she recognized. The Trickster's smile graced his face. *Do not ignore this. Do not pretend it didn't happen. Loki is here. In Jack.*

Verity turned to face Jack and lifted his hand to her breast while the other went around his neck to draw him in for a kiss. He fondled her over her shirt, sneaking it up to get to bare flesh.

She cupped his balls. He was already hard. She spoke plainly. "I want you. Now." She dropped to her knees before him and unfastened his belt. She reached inside his fly as she unzipped his jeans and slid her fingers into the slit of his shorts. She wrapped her fingers around his cock and pulled it forward, then, kneeling in the dirt before a tree dedicated to the goddess of the crossroads, she performed fellatio.

She realized she might be experiencing the most erotic moment of her life, to date. His magnificent cock felt good—felt right—in her mouth. She knew it. She knew Jack knew it. This was not a mundane blowjob. This—this act—was truly sacred sex. An oral communion of mouth to member, the cock telling the mouth what to do by how it grew harder and more engorged from long, deep strokes or a hand stroking the shaft, cupping the balls or fingers simply wrapped and squeezing.

Verity tasted Jack's salt. She pulled her mouth away with one long slurp and rested against her heels. She pulled off her shirt and moved her bare breasts closer to his erection. She stroked him off, and he shot hot onto her bosom.

"Fuck. I never want to be without your lips around my dick." Jack helped her to her feet and wiped away his semen with a napkin from dinner he'd stashed in his pocket. "But now, my dear—it's your turn." He held her close and kissed her. He pressed his tongue forward and tasted his musk from her mouth. He pulled up a handful of her skirt until he could comfortably slip a hand inside. Verity spread her stance for him. "We forgot the condom. Allow me to feel your orgasm against my fingertips."

Verity kissed his throat and moved her hips in time to his caressing, probing fingers. *I am so ready; so ready to come. He could use a Brillo pad on me and I'd still climax.* She lifted her chin and barely stifled a cry of ecstasy. She forced her eyes to stay open, for the Milky Way was above her head, and even in the height of her pleasure, she wanted to capture the heavenly visage with this moment.

Jack didn't remove his hand from her quim until the last quake of orgasm subsided. "Are you good?" he asked.

"Yes."

"Let's head back then. It certainly grew dark quickly."

"Look at the stars, Jack. The building is far away enough and there are very few surface lights around here. The Milky Way blessed us tonight." She pulled on her shirt and straightened her clothes as Jack tucked his member away and then zipped up.

"I think the gods, themselves, blessed us, when they brought Johnny and Chari together."

Verity felt the same way but wasn't sure how to respond. It was easier to share body parts than emotions. *We've known each other for a little over four hours and I feel like we have been a matched set for years.* "I am grateful. Even if we walk away from this and don't meet up later, I am grateful."

"I fully intend on seeing you again. I've been alone for a long time. My job has kept me traveling for years. With the opportunity to stay put for a year, I'm going to put down roots. Technically, I am an independent contractor and could teach online for any university program out there. I could go back to work for the Catholic Church. They have a huge research department. Of course, they bury most findings under dogma."

"I have not had a gentleman caller for a decade. Dates? Sure. Male friends? Of course. But someone I want to..."

Jack finished her sentence. "Have and hold?"

"Yeah. That. No one."

"I volunteer as tribute," Jack said, quoting from the popular movie *Hunger Games*.

Verity broke up laughing. "I love living vicariously through movie quotes."

"It's a game the whole family can play. Johnny and I used to sing the He-Man cartoon song as a bedtime prayer. Made our mother crazy."

"Charity and I tormented our mother similarly. Except mother was a swamp witch from the deep south and would get her hackles up when we'd ask to go to church with our friends—which we did only to annoy her."

"You were wicked little shits, huh? I hope my children will be kinder souls than I ever was." Jack reached for her hand.

"You have children?" she asked.

"Not yet."

"Do you want children?"

"I do."

Verity squeezed his hand. "So do I."

"I feel a tad bit apprehensive about what my brother and your sister are going to say as we sashay into the restaurant and tiptoe up the stairs to the temple."

"I'm feeling ya there, Jack." Verity flashed the time on her cell phone. "Wow. We are very late."

"I say we don't interrupt the ritual and maybe grab some leftovers from the kitchen and head back to the hobbit house. Watch Netflix." Jack paused, thoughtfully. "Tonight's temple is all about welcoming the gods and beginning a long service to spirit and human, reviving the intimacy between them. I think we got that covered."

"Fuck. Chari should use that in a brochure," Verity replied.

"You like that?"

"Yes. Very much."

"You bring out my inner poet."

The woods and field were dark, and their path barely lit from the soft glow of candles in the temple windows. The restaurant's kitchen lights were on, though the dining area was dark, except for a couple of emergency lights at the base of the stairwell.

They slipped into the kitchen and immediately broke out in laughter. "Oh, my gods! Johnny, you sly son of a bitch."

"Would you look at that." Verity picked up a fabric shopping bag tagged with her name. "They packed us a picnic."

Jack read the note pinned to his sack aloud. "Dear Jack, way to go, brother. Don't break her heart."

Verity giggled. "Well, listen to your brother, Jack." She held up Chari's note to her. "Dear Ver, I'm pretty impressed with the result of your participating in a little *old-time religion*. You honor the gods—they honor you right back. Congrats. I hope Jack is *the one*."

"Well, our siblings are running with this, aren't they?" It was far more a statement than a question.

"Jack, they can say whatever they want. We are big kids. We can make our own decisions." Verity pulled up a chair.

"I don't know if I deserve the title of *the one*, but I hope I'm at least somewhere near the top. I'd like this relationship to continue. I know we spoke about meeting up since I'm going to be in state working for a while—I hope this happens. I am very much enjoying the physical relationship we are having, and with every conversation we have, I find I am more and more attracted to you, overall."

"I would very much like to continue this relationship. On all levels."

Jack extended his hand to her. "Let's take these lovely bags of leftovers and wine back to the hobbit house."

AS QUIET AS THEY WERE, Chari knew Jack and Verity were in the building, and by the sounds of their footfalls, were leaving. She held a pink candle in a holder lined with rose petals, chocolate, ground coffee, and drops of holy water. She crept to the top of the staircase and sat. As Jack and Verity left the building, she snuffed out the candle and whispered into the smoke, "Intimacy, revived."

Johnny sat next to Charity. "Think your spell worked?"

"Oh, baby...I give good love spells. Especially where only a little nudge is needed."

About the Author

Darragha Foster is the author of the award-winning paranormal romance novel, *The Orca King*, as well as several other novels of a similar nature. She loves scary movies, her miniature dachshund, and her iPhone (which she claims changed her life). She has been married for over twenty years to her mate from the infinite past, a very patient man who doesn't mind being her crash-test dummy for love scenes. Her favorite quote is from the writings of Nichiren Daishonin: *Many raging fires are quenched by a single shower of rain.* Darragha is all about joy, and hopes she shares a bit of the same with her readers at every turn of the electronic page.

Printed in the USA
CPSIA information can be obtained
at www.ICGtesting.com
CBHW071245030624
9486CB00009B/144